ACCUSE THE TOFF

ACCUSE THE TOFF

John Creasey

CHIVERS
THORNDIKE

This Large Print book is published by BBC Audiobooks Ltd, Bath, England and by Thorndike Press®, Waterville, Maine, USA.

Published in 2005 in the U.K. by arrangement with Tethered Camel Publishing

Published in 2005 in the U.S. by arrangement with Tethered Camel Ltd.

U.K. Hardcover ISBN 1–4056–3262–3 (Chivers Large Print)
U.K. Softcover ISBN 1–4056–3263–1 (Camden Large Print)
U.S. Softcover ISBN 0–7862–7423–9 (Nightingale)

The text of this Large Print edition is unabridged.
Other aspects of the book may vary from the original edition.

Set in 16 pt. New Times Roman.

Printed in Great Britain on acid-free paper.

British Library Cataloguing in Publication Data available

Library of Congress Cataloging-in-Publication Data

Creasey, John.
    Accuse the Toff / by John Creasey.
        p.   cm.
    ISBN 0–7862–7423–9 (lg. print : sc : alk. paper)
    1. Toff (Fictitious character)—Fiction. 2. Private investigators—England—Fiction. 3. Large type books. I. Title. II. Series.
PR6005.R517A65 2005
823'.912—dc22   2004029248

FOREWARD

RICHARD CREASEY

The Toff—or the Honourable Richard Rollison—was 'born' in the twopenny weekly *Thriller* in 1933 but it was not until 1938 that my father, John Creasey, first published books about him. At once the Toff took on characteristics all his own and became a kind of *"Saint* with his feet on the ground." My father consciously used the Toff to show how well the Mayfair man-about-town could get on with the rough diamonds of the East End.

What gives the Toff his ever-fresh, ever-appealing quality is that he likes people and continues to live a life of glamour and romance while constantly showing (by implication alone) that all men are brothers under the skin.

I am delighted that the Toff is available again to enchant a whole new audience. And proud that my parents named me Richard after such an amazing role-model.

Richard Creasey is Chairman of The Television Trust for the Environment *and, for the last 20 years, has been an executive producer for both BBC and ITV.*

It was John Creasey who introduced him to

the world of travel and adventure. Richard and his brother were driven round the world for 465 days in the back of their parents' car when they were five and six years old. In 1992 Richard led 'The Overland Challenge' driving from London to New York via the Bering Strait.

CHAPTER ONE

A SOLDIER RUNS AMOK

'I'll bet he's tough,' said the bus conductor admiringly. 'You've got to hand it to them Commando boys, yes sir, you've got to hand it to them.' He watched the thick-set man in battle-dress move across the pavement after jumping from the bus then rang the bell for the driver to start off. Peering through the gloom of the winter evening he lost sight of the Commando, shrugged and added: 'I'll bet he's tough,' to a disinterested audience of passengers whose chief preoccupation was getting home before it grew really dark.

'I'll bet he is,' he repeated and clucked his tongue at the lack of response.

The soldier who had inspired the conductor's enthusiasm walked rapidly along the Chiswick High Road, intent on his progress, shouldering aside two or three people who were in his way: from them he earned approbrium, not blessings, but it was doubtful whether he heard them. Even at close quarters it was too dark for casual passers-by to see his face although they could discern the outlines of his revolver holster and the three stripes on his arms.

A clock in a nearby shop, where the shutters

1

were being put up, struck six.

The sergeant hurried on and, had the light been better, many would have seen a strained expression on his face as if he were afraid of being late for an appointment of great importance.

He reached a side-street near Turnham Green and swung into it. From the several shops on the left-hand side of the road people were emerging, more shutters were being put into position and from one a chink of light showed; vivid in the blackout.

A car pulled into the kerb.

The sergeant was walking on the edge of the pavement and jumped to one side as a wing brushed against him. He turned round and rasped:

'What the hell do you think you're doing?'

'I say, old boy, I *am* sorry,' said a plump little man at the driving-wheel. 'No damage, eh? That's good, that's good—'

He broke off, his voice ending on a gurgling note. His eyes were goggling towards the sergeant's right hand as the Commando snatched his revolver from its holster. The driver did not raise another shout, just flung himself to one side.

The roar of a revolver shot broke the quiet, hitherto disturbed only by hurrying footsteps and closing doors. A single flash of flame showed the car, the Commando and the driver who was slumping sideways. Someone

2

screamed; three or four people stopped indeterminately. One man, bolder than the rest, ran forward. The Commando swung round on him and fired again. The bold pedestrian gasped, staggered back and then began to shout:

'Police! Police!'

Half a dozen others took up the cry. The Commando peered about then jumped towards the car and pulled the driver towards him; the conductor had been right, the man was tough. He hauled the driver on to the pavement, sending him sprawling to the ground, then jumped into the driver's seat.

Not far off a police whistle shrilled out. Nearer at hand, four or five men came together from a small shop and the Commando fired towards them without apparent reason. The roar of the shots and the flashes of flame merged with the startled gasps of the men, three of whom fell.

A fourth darted back into the shop, a fifth took to his heels and ran.

The Commando started shouting at the top of his voice, uttering vicious and obscene oaths which made a grotesque anticlimax to the violence of his shooting. The engine of the car turned but three or four men gained enough courage to rush at him and two reached the running-board, one an officer in RAF uniform. He flung his revolver at them, striking one in the face, then lunged out and pushed the

3

second man into the road.

The Commando eased off the brakes while the RAF officer picked himself up, dusted his clothes, hesitated then turned and hurried away.

The car raced off, swerving past one cyclist but failing to avoid a second; there was a rending sound as a wing struck the back of a cycle, a scream as the cyclist went flying. The car passed the machine and rider, swung round a turning and then gathered speed. It had no lights and sent the traffic coming towards it into confusion. A policeman, knowing nothing of what had happened, bellowed and pointed towards the headlamps but the Commando ignored him. It was just light enough to see vague shapes and figures on the sidewalk while the lights from other cars and cyclists added to the glow. He wove in and out of the traffic, keeping his hand on the horn, sometimes emitting a high-pitched shout which made people stop and stare.

The headlamps of a car shone on him as it climbed a slight incline; in the eerie glow the sergeant's head was thrown well back, his mouth was wide open and he laughed with wild abandon.

Apparently he knew the road well. He swung across to take a right-hand turn, forcing another driver to jam on his brakes, a third car to bump into the one which had been forced to stop. The sergeant uttered a peal of fantastic

4

laughter then sent the stolen car along the street into which he had turned.

Two cars commandeered by the police flashed past the entrance to the turning; the policemen saw the cars which had bumped, suspected what had happened and stopped and turned, making inquiries and having their suspicions confirmed. But they were too late to get results for the Commando sergeant had disappeared.

There was no trace, that night, of the stolen car.

At the scene of the shooting were two ambulances, a doctor and a crowd which gathered in spite of the attempts of the police to clear it away. Rumours spread swiftly, the most fantastic that twenty people had been killed, the most conservative that a dozen had been shot. The truth was better even than that; seven people had been wounded, two of them fatally and a third so badly that whether he lived or died rested with the surgeons.

The only clue to the identity of the killer was the revolver and promptly the police made contact with the War Office. The effort to trace the gun to its user began.

Superintendent Grice of Scotland Yard said, with some scepticism, that they would be lucky if there were any news within a week. Grice could be forgiven both scepticism and pessimism for he conducted the inquiries that evening and interrogated the slightly wounded

5

as well as the spectators. All the stories were reasonably corroborative: the soldier had pushed his way through a crowd in the street, stepped to the edge of the pavement and been touched by the car. That slight mishap appeared to have turned his head for he had started the shooting then, haphazard and wild. Stories of his progress, after the shooting, of his high-pitched laughter—described by three people as demoniac—of his reckless driving, were carefully and painstakingly compiled.

By nine o'clock Grice had learned all he expected to and at long last consented to see the Press whose representatives were waiting with an eye on the clock. He gave them a story in a cold, precise fashion, leaving nothing out, and they went off fully satisfied. Already the national daily papers had sent reporters to seek first-hand personal stories of the *Commando Who Ran Amok* and, except for treatment and style, the stories which appeared in the various papers varied little. What was more surprising, the theories about the shooting were almost identical: a soldier had gone mad and fired at random at all whom he had passed. The parallel between the sensation and another, near the same place but some twelve months before, was drawn by each writer and the front pages of every newspaper devoted a headline and a few paragraphs to a subject only indirectly connected with the war. Another coincidence was widely reported. In the office above the shop a man named Ryson had been murdered two years before but the murderer had never been caught.

Amongst the millions of people in London who read the story was the Hon Richard Rollison. He read it more closely than most while drinking morning tea and sitting up in bed at his Gresham Terrace flat. He scanned two other versions, then heard the water running for his bath. He climbed thoughtfully out of bed and took his bath without making a comment to Jolly, his man, who was preparing breakfast. It was very cold and he saw frost on the roofs of houses nearby.

It was a source of considerable irritation to Rollison that he had been given a staff appointment at Whitehall. That the appointment carried with it the acting rank of Colonel did not appease him for he was a man who preferred an active life and a desk at Whitehall was no place for physical action. On the other hand his domicile in London, after two years either abroad or with his regiment in England, was a positive joy to Jolly.

That morning Rollison was not contemplating the office with the gloom which nearly always pervaded the beginning of his day. Generally speaking, that gloom only existed before he reached and after he left the office for he was kept busy and he did not look kindly upon those who condemned all red tape and Brass Hats and those who did not take an active part in the fighting. He had no set notions about work being done behind the scenes; his prejudice was against his own part in it.

With the case of the *Commando Who Ran Amok* fresh in his mind, he approached the small breakfast-room—in reality an alcove off the sitting-room-cum-study—with something approaching relish. Jolly, thin, of medium height and with a perpetually gloomy expression heightened by the deep lines engraven on his face, was waiting by the hotplate. Rollison joined him, standing half a head taller, still showing something of the tan of Libyan sun—he had left North Africa long before the battle of Egypt had begun—a dark-haired, good-looking man with a thin dark moustache and a square, clear-cut chin. His tan made his teeth seem even whiter than they were. He did not comment upon the morsel of fish to be followed by an even smaller morsel of bacon and a generous helping of mushrooms but said:

'You could go on and on doing this, Jolly, couldn't you? Getting my tea, running my bath, cooking my breakfast—my oath, I wonder you don't pick it up and throw it at me one day.'

'I should certainly not jeopardise a good situation, sir,' said Jolly, in whose melancholy eyes was a glimmer of a smile. 'Will you have

8

coffee or tea this morning?'

'There you go,' deplored Rollison. 'Not a single variation from the exasperating norm. Tea. Have you read the papers?'

'I glanced at them, sir.' Jolly deposited a plate on the table-mat and Rollison sat down. 'I'll go and make the tea, sir.' He went into the kitchen and Rollison propped the *Echo* in front of him and read of the mad Commando again, thoughtfully, and with one eyebrow raised above the other.

Jolly returned with tea, and said: 'A very nasty business at Chiswick last night, sir.'

'Ye-es,' admitted Rollison.

'I suppose they'll catch the poor fellow soon,' said Jolly. Rollison stared up at him, surprised.

'Poor fellow? The killer?'

'Madness is surely a thing to pity, sir.'

'H'm, yes,' said Rollison. 'So are the other poor beggars. Are you going to be busy this morning?'

'No more than usual, sir.'

'Good. Don't worry about lunch, I'll have it at the Club. Pop along to Green Road, Chiswick, and have a look at the scene of the doings, will you? There should be plenty of people about who can tell you just where it happened.'

'You don't think—' began Jolly.

'I don't think anything about it,' declared Rollison firmly. 'I'm curious, and have a

9

nostalgic yearning. Just that and no more. If there were no war I'd be there myself.'

'If there were no war there would be no Commandos,' said Jolly logically.

'There would be men and guns,' Rollison reminded him darkly. 'You won't be looking for anything in particular but just getting an impression of what happened there last night. You might even try to contact one or two of the eye-witnesses. The driver of the car, for instance, wasn't badly hurt. A bullet grazed the top of his head, according to the *Echo*, and just shaved his hair, according to the *Post*. His name's Ibbetson, a good North Country name suggesting a blunt man. Have a chat with him if you can and,' added Rollison grandly, 'pretend that there's no war, that I'll be along soon, that the Commando didn't go mad but did it on purpose. Start off on that premise and see where it takes you.'

'Is that wise, sir?' asked Jolly, eyeing his employer squarely.

'Why shouldn't it be?' demanded Rollison.

'You'll remember advising me always to beware of the false premise,' said Jolly. 'And in any case, sir, supposing by some remote chance there is more in it than meets the eye, you aren't likely to have an opportunity to do anything constructive.'

'There is never any opportunity at all unless you make it yourself,' declared Rollison. 'Don't moralise, mobilise!' He smiled, lighting

10

a cigarette after finishing the mushrooms and while contemplating his second cup of tea. 'You may be right. You usually are and, when I get home tonight, I'll probably have forgotten it. But have a full report, will you, particularly from Mr Ibbetson.'

As it transpired he did not forget the affair when he reached the office; and it happened that a batch of correspondence he expected to find waiting for him had been delayed and would not arrive until the afternoon. As that meant that he and the two members of his clerical staff would have to work well into the evening, he declared it fitting that they should take the morning off. He stayed in the office until half-past eleven then strolled along Whitehall thoughtfully, reaching Parliament Street and nodding towards a constable beating his arms about his chest while standing outside the iron gates of Scotland Yard. The constable smiled in turn and saluted and Rollison turned his steps towards the Yard. Determining that there was no sense at all in asking whether Superintendent Grice was in and, in any case, convinced that Grice would not have anything to tell him beyond what he read in the newspapers, so that a visit would be a waste of time, he reached the constable who wished him a bright good morning and said that it was cold.

'Hallo,' said Rollison amiably. 'Is Mr Grice in?'

11

'He came in about half an hour ago, sir.'

Rollison decided that the Fates were conspiring in his favour. 'I'll go and have a chat with him, I think.' He nodded and passed by, not hearing the question of a youthful-looking constable who approached the man to whom Rollison had talked and asked:

'Who's that fellow, Joe?'

'Who, him?' asked Joe. '*That's* Mr Rollison.'

'Never 'eard of him,' declared the other.

'Never 'eard—heard—of Mr Rollison?' Joe, florid and grey in the Yard's service, stared at the man aghast. 'Now listen, young feller-me-lad, don't try jokes on me. *And* remember yer aitches. If yer want to get on in the Force you've got to speak well, see? Don't take any notice of some of the old-timers who've got on even though they drop their aitches; things are different now.'

'Okay, okay,' said the younger man impatiently. 'I can't help forgetting now and again. But who is *he*?' As he saw Joe's expression of gathering wrath, he added hastily. 'Go on, I mean it, I've never 'eard of 'im.'

'You've never 'eard of the Toff?' demanded Joe, practice of his preaching going to the winds in sheer surprise. Then witheringly: 'And you call yerself a policeman!'

The younger man's eyes widened, his eyes kindled, there was a note of satisfaction in his voice.

12

'The *Toff*, is he? Strewth, he's the bloke who helped old Gricey bottle up the black market.' He peered towards the doorway which had swallowed Rollison while for some moments Joe was silent. Then, with heavy emphasis, the older man said:

'That's who he is. But not so much of the 'Old Gricey' when you're on duty, you never know who's passing here. Morning, sir,' he added, as a dapper man passed with a brief nod. Then, *sotto voce*: 'Yer see? That's the Super from X Division, Chiswick; he might have heard and I'll bet he's going to see Superintendent Grice now. I wonder what's up?' added Joe reminiscently. 'When the Toff blows in, something nearly always happens. I wouldn't half like to be at that "chat" he's having with Gricey.'

'Now, Joe,' said the younger man reprovingly. 'You'll get overheard one of these days, talking disrespectful of the Super. You never know who's passing by.'

Joe glowered at him and stepped to the other side of the gate, thinking less of his spell of duty on guard than of the Toff and the stories which had built themselves up about that almost legendary figure.

CHAPTER TWO

LITTLE PATCHES OF ICE

Superintendent Grice, tall, academic of appearance with a high forehead and large brown eyes, looked up when the door of his room opened and then started to his feet. He was dressed immaculately in brown and his smile of welcome emphasised the peculiar way in which his skin stretched across his nose and his cheeks, giving them an almost transparent look although he was not over-thin.

'Hallo, Rollison,' he said with warmth and offered a hand. 'What's brought you?'

'Idleness, sloth and a delayed mail,' Rollison answered. 'I mean I had half an hour to spare. You're looking well.'

'I've never seen you looking better,' returned Grice and pulled up a chair. 'Now that the pleasantries are over, what has brought you?' He regarded the Toff expectantly: his manner said as clearly as Joe's words that he did not believe that the Toff had come simply for the sake of a visit.

Rollison chuckled.

'I've said my piece.'

'You're an evasive beggar,' declared Grice; 'but I suppose I mustn't try to alter you.' He stretched back in his chair and locked his fingers behind his neck. 'So without any ulterior motive you came in, just for the sake of a talk about old times. You wouldn't waste my time. You've a fair idea of how busy I am.'

'Picture of a policeman hard at work,' murmured the Toff, regarding the half-recumbent figure with some amusement. 'Seriously, I—' he paused and then shrugged. 'I suppose if the truth were known, I'm intrigued by the Chiswick business.'

Although the Superintendent did not alter his position or make any comment there was a noticeable alteration in his expression. His eyes narrowed a little and his lips tightened. He was balancing precariously on the back legs of his chair, swaying gently to and fro.

Then: 'Intrigued?' he said heavily.

'Just that.'

'You aren't natural,' declared Grice and brought the front legs of his chair down so that in a moment he was sitting upright at the desk. 'Why on earth should it intrigue you? A man who's been trained to the limit, living under a considerable strain—you'd assume that, as he's a Commando—cracks up and goes haywire. It's happened often enough before. Now and again there's an unsuspected neurotic amongst the special troops and it comes out when least expected. Why shouldn't it be just that?'

'Isn't it?' murmured the Toff.

Grice raised one eyebrow above the other. 'It wouldn't surprise me to hear that you know

15

damned well that it isn't,' he said. 'Or it mightn't be,' Grice corrected slowly. 'It was a peculiar business and I haven't sorted it out yet. On the surface everything is the same as it's been before. The last straw breaking the camel's back, a wild shooting affray and a mad rush by car. The main difference is that the man got away this time, evading all his followers. We've traced most of the eye-witnesses—in fact the only one who was there but hasn't been found was a young RAF man. He'll probably keep in the background.'

'So I read,' said Rollison.

'What did you read into it?' asked Grice, obviously genuinely interested in the other's opinions.

'Just a single question,' Rollison admitted. 'Here's a man who goes haywire after a slight jolt from a car, sprays bullets about him and then tears off in the said car. But he doesn't dash along the main road until he has a crash; he doesn't do the things that a man suffering from a brainstorm is likely to. He goes down a narrow turning leading to a maze of streets— I'm quoting the *Echo*—and disappears completely. He could have turned off at several other points but without a maze of streets conveniently handy for losing himself in.'

He broke off and regarded the Superintendent with some eagerness while Grice nodded.

16

'I've got that far,' he admitted. 'Just.'

'Have you found the car yet?' asked Rollison.

'Yes. Stranded near the Grand Junction Canal, at Wembley,' Grice told him. 'We're having the canal dragged. It's just possible that he came to, realised what he'd done and drowned himself. But there's an odd thing,' added the Superintendent. 'The canal is patrolled regularly by the Home Guard and a man who passed the spot at six o'clock this morning swears that it wasn't there then. Another, who passed at eight—on the last round, they only patrol it during darkness—discovered it. The petrol tank,' he added heavily, 'was half-full.'

Rollison's eyes narrowed.

'The man Ibbetson said it was only a quarter-full when it was stolen. Quoting the *Post*!'

'You don't miss much,' admitted Grice. 'I haven't made up my mind whether Ibbetson knew there was more petrol in the tank than there should have been and is covering himself or whether the car was taken somewhere else and refilled. It might have travelled a hundred miles during the night: Ibbetson says he doesn't remember the mileage showing when it was stolen.'

He paused and then the telephone rang on his desk. He lifted it and after a moment said: 'Ask him to come along, will you?' He replaced the receiver and added: 'The police-surgeon who treated the victims is coming in with the Chiswick man who's upstairs with Freeman. Stay, if you'd care to.'

'I don't think I'll worry,' said Rollison, pushing his chair back. 'There is one other little thing—'

'Let it come,' invited Grice.

'Who died?' asked Rollison. 'Did they matter? Could they have been picked out?'

Grice rubbed his long chin.

'One was a customer, the other a member of the staff of a shop in Green Road—a furniture shop. The other members of the staff, three in all, were leaving at the same time, just after six o'clock. They were in a group in the doorway and the staff usually leaves at six o'clock promptly, so that it could have been prearranged. On the other hand, Ibbetson wasn't concerned with the shop or any of the people there. Nor were others who were wounded. If the shots were intended for the group coming from the shop, several were wasted beforehand. It was too dark for our man to distinguish one from the other. Everything considered, I'd say that the shooting was haphazard but that isn't conclusive.'

'As far as I can see we've reached the same stage,' said Rollison. 'It could be a genuine case of *dementia* or there might be deep things beyond it. I suppose we'll see,' he added and smiled lazily as he rose to his feet. 'On what part of the Grand Junction Canal was the car parked?'

'The stretch of bank between Wembley and Willesden,' Grice told him. 'Are you going out there?'

'Do you know,' said Rollison earnestly, 'I feel that a breath of fresh air would do me good. But I've only a couple of hours to spare and it's an exercise in curiosity more than anything else. If I should see anything that looks interesting I'll give you a ring when I'm back.'

'Thanks,' said Grice; and meaningly: 'Don't forget.'

The door opened as Rollison reached it, to admit the dapper man whom Joe had commented upon and another. They exchanged nods and Rollison went out, walking along the high-ceilinged passages of the Yard to the courtyard and thence to Westminster Underground Station. It was obvious that Grice had ideas similar to his own about the shooting affray. Grice was a level-headed and logical man and between the two of them there was both understanding and respect.

On the way to Wembley, Rollison alternated between moods of pleasure and satisfaction at being involved, even tentatively, in a case that was at least intriguing and depressed at the realisation that the pressure of work at the office was too great for him to devote much time to it. By the time he reached the canal, finding a taxi near Wembley Station which deposited him outside a narrow alleyway leading to the waterway, he decided that this one mission of inquiry should be his last but he also wondered what would be said if he put in an application for a few days' leave. He had received none for six months, not even a long weekend. Arguing that he had every justification for such a request, he saw the small Ford standing against wooden fencing which divided the canal bank from some allotments. Three policemen were near the car—a grey one—while two small boats were moving along the canal, the end of a long drag-net fastened to each. Three men were in each boat and all seemed intent on their task, although obviously perished by the cold.

The January sun was bright and clear; white frost still covered the ground where there was shadow and the grass of the paths on the allotments looked wet and fresh. The air was crisp, invigorating as wine. He strolled along thoughtfully while the police on the bank eyed him curiously. One of them recognised him and Rollison heard his name passed on to the others. That saved him the need of explanations and he exchanged greetings with the sergeant in charge then strolled along, watching the boats on their grim task and seeing the wide, earth-surfaced towpath going

20

along in a straight line for half a mile or more. Round a corner in the canal he saw the chimneys of a house, divorced from the roof and showing above a large bill-posting board; wisps of smoke rose from them and were carried straight up, for there was no wind.

Half-way between the Ford and the chimneys he slipped.

He had been walking carelessly and had not noticed a small puddle, ice-covered, near the canal. His heel skidded on it and he clawed the air to keep his balance and save himself from falling. Instead he hastened his fall and lurched sideways towards the unruffled surface of the canal. Someone shouted: 'Look out!' Rollison's heart turned over and he leaned his weight towards the towpath but, for a moment, thought a ducking unavoidable. He even prepared to make a deliberate plunge rather than go in accidentally and risk twisting himself but, with a last-minute effort, brought himself to a standstill on the edge of the water. His hat fell from his head as he did so and dropped straight into the canal, splashing water up into his face.

As he backed from the icy patch one of the policemen hurried up, carrying a small pole. He retrieved the hat and Rollison, profuse with thanks, left it on the bank to dry, congratulating himself on evading a wetting. Then he peered thoughtfully at the puddle and another a yard farther away while the

21

policeman reassured himself that Rollison was all right and went back to the car.

Rollison looked at the row of puddles, frowned and glanced along the bank. There was an edging of concrete all along it and, at regular intervals, small rings where boats could be tied. Some three yards from the first ice-covered puddle was a coating of ice upon the concrete; it spread for several feet in either direction, narrowing as it encroached farther on the path itself.

'Odd,' murmured Rollison audibly.

He walked back a few yards and then turned. The sun shone on the coating of ice and the puddles which stretched for several yards at evenly spaced intervals, growing smaller until they seemed to disappear altogether. He walked along again, stepping more carefully. Watching his feet, he saw that from the first puddle to the second there was the distance of a normal stride—as long as his own, suggesting a tall man—and that the puddles were spaced at similar intervals.

He looked round to find the sergeant close on his heels again. A thick-set man with a ruddy complexion and a sober expression, the man eyed Rollison without a smile and asked:

'Have you noticed anything, sir?'

'I'm not sure,' replied Rollison evasively. 'Have you?'

'I can't say that I have,' admitted the sergeant.

'Wait here for a few minutes, will you?' asked Rollison. 'I'll be back.' He walked on with a faster but still cautious stride, watching the ground. At regular intervals there were the faint traces of ice on the ground. The farther he went the fainter the traces became until they looked little more than patches of white frost.

Standing by the last, he looked up and saw the small house perhaps twenty yards away. It was a cottage, creeper-clad with an evergreen, looking charming and picturesque, out of place against a background of factory chimneys and large buildings and, farther distant, the red tops of a vast mass of little houses. There was a well-tended garden, a shed, a small coal-house. It was the home of a man who took pride in it and who also took great pains with the outside for there was fresh paint at the windows and the door. The curtains looked clean, suggesting a housewife as proud as her spouse.

On either side of the narrow gate leading to it were high privet hedges, sheared into round balls and casting shadows over the gate itself. Rollison reached the gate and looked at the top rail; on it was a smear of ice. He put his hand on the smear, finding that his span covered it. Stepping back, he saw an icicle dripping from the bar immediately below the patch; but for those things the gate was quite clear of ice.

'It's just possible,' murmured the Toff *sotto voce*. 'A man fell, jumped or was pushed into the river, clambered out—accounting for the first ice patch—walked along steadily after standing still for a moment and accounting for the pool and the second ice patch. As he walked the water dripped from his trousers at first and made the other pools but when it stopped dripping there was no water and therefore no ice. But he came here and gripped the gate with his hand; his hand was wet from his clothes. More water, which dripped and froze and became an icicle. The perfect reconstruction!' He smiled sardonically and rubbed his chin, glancing again towards the house.

A movement at a window in the roof, a little attic window, attracted him. For a moment he glimpsed the face of a man, no more than a youth: he had a vivid impression of staring eyes and drawn lips; then the face disappeared but the white curtains continued to move.

Rollison half-turned and called to the sergeant: 'There's nothing here, I'm afraid,' saying so deliberately because he did not want the man to approach.

As he saw the sergeant turn away he heard the front door of the cottage opening and he looked over his shoulder. An old, grey-haired man in shirt-sleeves braved the cold of the day to walk quickly along the path. Rollison turned back and watched him. A lined face, weather-

24

beaten by constant exposure, held bright blue eyes which were both angry and anxious. Rollison thought that the other's lips were a little unsteady as he asked:

'Do—do you want anything, sir?'

Rollison smiled at him charmingly and took out his cigarette-case. He proffered it and the old man said that he did not mind if he did; his fingers were unsteady as he extracted a cigarette. Rollison flicked his lighter into flame.

'I was going to find out whether I could get a cup of tea,' he admitted. 'I've walked much farther than I intended and—' he broke off, his smile widening. 'Then I decided that it wouldn't be fair with rationing and all that.' He raised a hand, a resigned gesture.

It wouldn't be any *trouble*,' said the old man but he had some difficulty in articulating. 'I don't know how mother's fixed for tea, though.' He stood indeterminate, eyeing the Toff and further convincing the latter that he was anxious although the anger had faded from his eyes. 'Shall I go and ask her?'

'Would you mind?' asked Rollison. 'It would be a kindly act if she did make one.' He opened the gate and saw the old man lick his lips. A step behind the other he walked up the garden path with a trim privet hedge on either side of him. Glancing up to the attic window he saw the curtains move again.

A sharp gasp greeted his entry into the

parlour of the cottage; the front door led straight into the room where he saw a kitchen dresser. A swift movement followed and then a clatter of pots and pans; something broke. Rollison made a banal comment while the old man hurried into the kitchen. Another gasp and a tearful voice was raised on a high note to be cut short by a gruff command from the man. A whisper which followed came clearly:

'You must pull yourself together, Jane! He's a decent chap, he wants . . .'

The words faded while Rollison drew on his cigarette and then glanced out of the door by which he had entered. It led, on the far side, to another room and a flight of stairs. He stepped towards the stairs and ascended them, making little sound. A small landing at the top revealed three doors and a loft-ladder; there was an opening in the ceiling—the entrance, he assumed, to the attic. He reached the ladder and began to mount it, still making hardly a sound, intent on his errand but prepared at any moment to hear an exclamation from below-stairs, evidence that he was missed.

No interruption came from the parlour but he heard a gasp above his head and then a bundle, which looked like clothes, hurtled down. He swayed to one side on the ladder; the bundle struck it, then dropped heavily to the floor. A moment later a pair of legs showed, feet rested on the top rung of the ladder and the man from the attic began to hurry down. He swung from the ladder ahead of Rollison, landed heavily, made a wild blow at Rollison and then darted for the stairs.

CHAPTER THREE

THE GUN IS TRACED

As Rollison evaded the wild swing a cry came from downstairs. At the same moment he saw the feverish eyes of the man who rushed past him, a good-looking youngster with lips drawn back over large white teeth. The youth ran for the stairs, the shouting from below grew in volume while Rollison followed more leisurely to the landing, taking his revolver from his holster as he went. The escapee was near the bottom step when Rollison called down:

'I shouldn't go any farther. I don't want to shoot.'

The casualness of the words made them effective. The youth stopped on the bottom step; instinctively his arms went upwards. Into the small passage crowded the old man and a woman, a tiny, thin creature with white hair and enormous, horrified eyes.

'Oh, Tom, Tom, Tom!' she incanted. 'Oh, Tom, Tom!' She pushed past her husband and reached the youth, flinging her arms about him. 'They won't hurt you, they won't! Oh, Tom!'

It was not a moment for sentiment or soft speaking although the poignancy of the scene was not lost on Rollison. He stood half-way down the stairs, still pointing his gun, and spoke sharply:

'Stand aside, mother! Don't play any foolish tricks, son, you'll only get hurt. Turn round and let me get a look at you.'

The boy obeyed.

He was dressed in an ill-fitting suit of navy blue. His eyes were blue and his face made it obvious that he was the son of the old man. His features were clear-cut and he was pleasant-looking despite the fear in his eyes and the way his mouth quivered. Yet he eyed the Toff steadily while he stood by his mother and his father joined them.

Looking down on them, Rollison wondered if ever there had been so odd a scene. Then he spoke firmly:

'I don't know what this is about yet but the quicker I do the better for all. Supposing you go in the parlour and sit down?' He went a step nearer them and they backed into the little parlour, furnished with old-fashioned furniture but not overloaded with knick-knacks or photographs. For the first time Rollison grew aware of an appetising smell coming from the kitchen; it reminded him that he was hungry. The trio obeyed and sat down.

The woman burst out quickly and tearfully, her right hand clutching her son's arm.

'He didn't mean it; he didn't, I tell you; my Tom wouldn't do such a thing! He was—he was going to give himself up, weren't you, Tom? Tell the officer you were, tell him! It's only been three days, he didn't mean to desert, I swear he didn't! He got drunk, he was out with a lot of men older than he is, and they made him drunk! He would have come back himself. I swear he would!'

She stopped abruptly, peering at the Toff as if trying to judge his reception of the statement. What the woman said could explain the family's anxiety and the youth who had been hiding. He looked again into the clear eyes of the soldier who would be classed a deserter and remembered the man who had run amok on the previous night. Sharpness would get him the necessary information quickly, sympathy would fail him.

'Where's your uniform?' he demanded.

'In—in the kitchen,' muttered the youth.

'What's your name?'

'J—Jameson, sir.'

'Regiment?'

'The—the Twenty-first Commando Detachment, sir.'

Commando, thought Rollison, and narrowed his eyes. But he did not allow the other a respite and fired question after question, getting straight answers to them all.

29

Jameson said that he had been on seven days' leave and was now three days overdue. He had been stationed in Kent. He had spent most of the leave with his parents but met a crowd of men he knew at a public-house three nights before. He had got drunk and did not remember what had happened until the following morning when he had arrived home in a condition so maudlin that he had been put to bed immediately. Then he had discovered that his revolver and some of his equipment was missing. Knowing the men with whom he had been drinking, he had gone to see them the next night, being assured that none of them had seen the missing equipment. Scared of reporting without it, he had tried again on the following night—the night of the shooting affray.

'I—I only had a bitter, sir,' he exclaimed, as he saw the apparently sceptical expression on Rollison's face. 'Just one, that's all! It—it knocked me over; I went right out, drunk as a lord. I'm not used to it, honestly I'm not, but I can't understand one—one bitter.'

'Nor will anyone else,' said Rollison uncompromisingly.

He felt that it was reasonably likely that the worry of the older Jamesons was simply that the youth had overstayed his leave and lost his equipment; he could not yet be certain of the youngster himself. He could understand, too, that they would look on deserting as a cardinal crime, could imagine the panic into which the youth's carousals had sent the household. But he was not interested in that, as such: he was interested in Jameson's gun and equipment.

'But it's true,' protested Jameson. 'I remember that clearly, and then—and then I don't remember anything else until I was in the water.'

'What water?'

'Why, the canal, sir,' exclaimed the old man. 'Tom was walking home, he must have been walking home, and fell in. That sobered him; he's not a lad who's ever taken much strong drink and he climbed out and came home. He was going to report, sir, I swear it! He wasn't going to waste no more time looking for his gun or anything, he was going back to his unit as—as soon as he'd got his clothes dried. We had them hanging in the kitchen but mother took them down when we saw you.'

'They're all bundled up in a cupboard now,' declared "mother" pathetically.

Rollison looked from one to the other. Young Jameson's manner impressed him favourably; the story of the lost gun and equipment was plausible enough to explain his first reluctance to return to his unit. To overstay leave was bad enough but to admit losing equipment would earn double punishment. It was a trivial business, even though it would appear enormous in the eyes of this family; but the point at issue was how it

31

affected the shooting in Chiswick. It was too much of a coincidence to believe that the car had been placed near the cottage quite independently of Jameson's return.

He decided it was time for the more sympathetic approach and he took out his cigarette-case again. Jameson looked startled when offered a cigarette but said 'No thank you, sir,' stiffly, as if expecting a rebuke if he accepted. The old man followed the son's example. Rollison lit a cigarette, leaned against an easy chair and spoke quietly:

'I want you to listen carefully, Jameson. Quite accidentally, I think'—the mendacity in the circumstances was justifiable—'you've become mixed up in something more than over-staying your leave. Have you told me the whole story without any frills or any lies?'

'It's God's truth, sir!'

'I hope so,' said Rollison slowly. 'The trouble I've mentioned is about a car that was stolen last night and found near here. Probably you've seen it.' The old man nodded and the woman gasped. 'I don't know a great deal about it but I can tell you that it was driven by a Commando.' Rollison skidded over thin ice expertly and went on: 'So before you report to your unit, Jameson, I want you to come with me and see the police in London.'

'But—' began Mrs Jameson aghast.

'The police!' exclaimed the old man.

It was Jameson himself who interrupted

their protests, eyeing Rollison with a sudden new interest, frowning a little but speaking with an eager note in his voice.

'Just a minute, mother. Would you mind telling me your name, sir?'

'Rollison,' said the Toff, and waited.

'I *thought* so,' said Jameson, softly, and there was a gleam in his eyes, eagerness in his expression. 'I've read a lot about you, sir, of course. Who hasn't? I'll come with you gladly. It'll be all right, mother,' he went on quickly. 'You've heard me talk of Mr Rollison. The Toff.' He uttered the soubriquet a little hesitantly, bringing a smile to Rollison's lips and a gasp of surprise from the old man.

Jameson, not Rollison, won the parents over to make no further protest, except that Mrs Jameson refused to let him leave without his dinner. She made so bold, she said, as to wonder if Colonel Rollison would care to share their humble meal. Rollison, mildly amused at the irony of the situation, feeling for the old folk, partly convinced of Jameson's sincerity and yet reserving final judgment on him, gladly joined them. The meal was as appetising as its aroma had promised and he did no more than justice to it while wondering what the police outside would have said had they known the whole truth.

Outside, the police were still dragging the canal.

Jameson passed them without comment.

33

Nor did he speak while they walked to the trams which ran nearby and boarded one for the nearest station. He was silent on the journey, also, and his first comment, except for odd, irrelevant remarks, came when their taxi drew up outside the doors of Scotland Yard.

'What am I wanted for, sir?'

'I don't know that you're wanted yet,' said Rollison. 'In any case, if you've told the truth you're all right.' He led the way to the waiting-room then asked Jameson to stay there until he was sent for. In the passage outside Rollison called a constable aside and asked him to make sure the other man did not leave then hurried along to Grice's office; the fact that he was *persona grata* at the Yard had rarely been more useful.

He tapped on Grice's door and put his head into the room. Grice was speaking into the telephone but glanced up and, when he saw the caller, beckoned him with his free hand. He continued speaking for some seconds then replaced the receiver and pushed the instrument away from him with a sigh.

'Aliens, aliens, nothing but aliens,' he complained. 'My life is a nightmare with 'em. It doesn't matter what job we're on, the Alien Laws crop up somewhere and there are times when I could do violence to the authors of 18B!' He smiled wryly and his mood altered. 'But never mind that, Rollison, I've some news about the shooting. The War Office has done a

34

remarkably good job this time.'

'Be careful,' warned Rollison. 'Remember I adorn it. What have they done?'

'Traced the gun back to its owner,' said trice. 'Or lessee, as the case may be. A Thomas Martin Jameson at Canal Cottage, Wembley.' The Superintendent's eyes were creased as he went on: 'You were right on his doorstep, Rolly. There's ttricehe car stranded nearby and a Commando living on the spot, one whose gun was used last night. I've put out a call for Jameson, of course, and his home will be visited this afternoon. We may find the explanation the simple one. Well, now—what did you find?' added Grice. 'It isn't a day I'd choose to walk along the canal for the sake of it.'

Rollison put his head on one side.

'Cancel the call for Jameson,' he urged. 'I have him with me, together with a story that fits all the questions we've been asking ourselves.' He paused long enough to survey and enjoy Grice's expression of sheer incredulity. 'Before I get back to the office I've just time for this. Jameson says that he was due to go back off leave, had a final night out, mixed with a hard-drinking crowd at a local pub and had too much to drink. His gun and other odds and ends were stolen. When he sobered up he was scared because he'd overstayed his leave and his parents are the kind to think the immediate penalty for desertion is shooting. He tried to get the gun back but failed. He tried again, was dosed with a knockout—that seems to be what happened, anyhow—and, later, thrown into the canal. The throwing coincided with the arrival of the Ford. The reason for it all is obvious. We were to believe that Jameson had a grouch and was worried. The incident with Ibbetson worried him more and he went off the handle, took the car, returned to a spot near his home, was filled with remorse and tried to drown himself. Impact with cold water removing his more distant fears, he climbed out and sought refuge at home. That,' finished Rollison, 'is the story. It looks pretty, doesn't it?'

Grice made no comment at all.

'Of course, Jameson may have done the job himself and thought this story up,' conceded the Toff. 'But if we grant that he did lose his gun and someone else used it, we have the perfect picture in the perfect frame—with one thing that went wrong; would Jameson, in such circumstances, drive right up to his own doorstep before trying to drown himself? On the face of it, I say no.'

CHAPTER FOUR

ROLLISON REMEMBERS IN TIME

'I don't say anything,' said Grice, after a long pause. 'I'm coming up for breath.' He eased his collar, leaned forward and implored: 'Tell me exactly what happened. I'm still trying to understand how you made contact with Jameson at all.'

Rollison told the story concisely while Grice made shorthand notes. As he talked, Rollison found his belief in Jameson strengthening at the same time as the case against the youngster appeared to harden. When he finished the recital he went on without a noticeable pause:

'Items to check: (a) What pub did Jameson go to? (b) Did he inquire about any lost equipment? (c) Who drank with him there? Answer those and you may be a long way on the road to solving the case. What is your reaction now?'

Slowly Grice rubbed his chin.

'I wouldn't like to say,' he admitted. 'I haven't your simple faith in the young man but I may be more inclined that way when I've seen him. He is here, isn't he?'

'He's here.' Rollison glanced at his watch. 'By George, it's nearly three. Be a kind soul and deal gently with Jameson for the time being, won't you? Oh—will you be here tonight?'

'What time do you mean?' demanded Grice.

'Around ten.'

'Probably I'll be here,' said Grice glumly, 'and if not you can get me at home. You must go, I suppose? I'd prefer you to have a word with Jameson with me.'

'Confound it, the war must go on,' declared Rollison, getting up and stepping to the door. 'But just at the moment, and for no reason at all, I'm holding a watching brief for Jameson. I'll be seeing you,' he promised, and hurried out.

He left Superintendent Grice frowning at the closed door and Grice was still frowning when Rollison opened it again to say:

'Did I tell you that he's in the waiting-room?'

Grice nodded.

Rollison reached his office to find two reproachful assistants waiting; some minor correspondence had been sorted and there was an air of suspended animation in the room. On the short journey from the Yard he had considered both Jameson's story and the probability that Grice suspected him of knowing more than he admitted; he put all contemplation of the affair out of his mind while he dealt with a welter of detail concerning mysterious matters of material and equipment in the mass.

One of the inevitable consequences of a large and widely dispersed army was that equipment was often in places where it should not be and urgently wanted where it should be. The greater part of the discrepancies were accidental; but some were deliberate and a thoughtful War Office had decided that Rollison was just the man to handle the cases of pilfering and/or major thefts within the various commands.

At five o'clock he had some tea in the office and dictated letters while drinking it. At half-past six he had five minutes to spare and wished that he had been back at the office at two o'clock promptly; as a consequence of the delay he would be lucky to get away before half-past ten and the 'staff' was still silently reproachful. Both girls were in their small ante room and two typewriters were going at full speed when the door opened and a tall, very fat man entered and closed the door with a bang. His uniform rode uneasily about his *embonpoint* and his trousers were too tight and too short.

Rollison affected to start.

'That's right, make me more jumpy than I am,' he protested. 'In a search for a few odd million rounds of ammunition which should be in Berkshire but aren't, some noises off are helpful. Bimble, may I resign?'

Lt Colonel d'Arcy Bimbleton uttered a

deep, rolling chuckle and followed with an unequivocal 'no'.

'Thanks,' said Rollison sardonically. 'In that case, don't come in and gloat because you're just going home and I shall be in this benighted sarcophagus for the next four hours.'

Bimbleton sat on the corner of Rollison's desk, his smile disappearing.

'I've often wondered just what is a sarcophagus,' he said earnestly. 'You don't happen to know, do you?'

'It's a coffin,' declared Rollison ghoulishly. 'Made of a stone that eats your flesh away as you lay in it. Don't stay here too long, Bimble, or you'll have to be refitted and refurnished.'

'Is it, by Jove!' exclaimed Bimbleton, sticking to the point. 'Interesting ideas some people have. Seriously, will you be late tonight? I thought you might like some snooker.'

'I shall be very late,' said Rollison firmly.

'It's partly your own fault,' Bimbleton told him. 'I know you weren't back from lunch until after three o'clock. I was here about three. Nothing that mattered, your girl fixed me up. Useful little girl, by the way, she—'

'Has no time for affairs of heart,' declared Rollison. 'She's already engaged to a handsome young Flight Lieutenant.' He leaned back in his chair and put his head on one side before he added thoughtfully: 'What

40

chance do you think I have of getting a week's leave?'

Bimbleton started, aghast, considered for a while, then very slowly and deliberately declared that Rollison would probably get it if he asked for it; only a lunatic would ask at the present juncture and lunatics were not in demand. Bimbleton continued in that strain until a typist brought in letters for Rollison's signature. When she had gone he removed his bulk from the desk and said off-handedly:

'As a matter of fact, Rolly, I looked in to ask you why you were at the Yard this morning. Saw you go in. Any connection between that and you wanting to leave? No? I'm not curious,' added Bimbleton hurriedly, seeing the gleam in Rollison's eyes. 'I just wondered, that's all. Cheerio, old man, I won't delay you. So long!' He raised a hand, and inserted himself into the narrow aperture to which he opened the door and then peered smilingly back. 'You know where to come if you want any help.'

'I wonder how many others saw me go there?' murmured Rollison as the door closed and he pulled the sheaf of letters towards him.

Just before ten o'clock his desk was clear and the typists were dabbing powder on their faces before venturing into the blackout. They stopped as Rollison entered the ante room but he signalled to them to go on; they finished sketchily as Rollison said:

41

'If everyone here did as good a job as you two, we'd have a lot to be thankful for. Good night.'

He did not hear their flattering remarks as they hurried together along the passages but sat back in his chair and deliberated on the wisdom of going to see Grice. He was tired and his eyes were heavy. He locked his desk, deferring a decision on whether to go to the Yard or to the flat; eventually the flat won but he felt too jaded to wonder seriously whether Jolly had had a fruitful morning at Chiswick, deciding that in all likelihood it had been a waste of time. Stripped of irrelevancies, adornments, romancing and improbability, the situation resolved itself to elementary simplicity. Young Jameson had been scared of returning to his unit, had drunk himself to a state of dt's, gone berserk, realised and repented it and also recovered sufficiently to present a good story.

When Rollison learned from Jolly that the mission to Chiswick had indeed been fruitless and that the man Ibbetson had added nothing to what the papers reported, Rollison decided that the elementary simplicity was on the mark, consoled himself with a weak whisky-and-soda and regaled Jolly with the story of the midday adventure, followed by his conclusions.

Jolly heard him out, kept silent for some seconds afterwards and then declared flatly:

42

'You'll feel better in the morning, sir. Do you think an early night is advisable?'

Rollison eyed him severely.

'And just what inspired that remark, Jolly?'

'It was just a passing comment,' Jolly assured him smoothly. 'Your eyes look very heavy, sir; I think perhaps you're sickening for a cold. Shall I put a hot water bottle in your bed?'

'Not tonight, nor any night,' said Rollison roundly. 'What you mean is that if Jameson is the man it's all too simple. I suppose it is. See if Grice is in the office, will you?'

Jolly telephoned the Yard and then Grice's Fulham home; the Superintendent was at neither place. Dissatisfied with himself, disgruntled and at heart wondering whether a hot water bottle would not have been a good idea after all, Rollison was in bed by half-past eleven and asleep before midnight.

He was aware of a disturbance in the flat some time afterwards but so long had passed since disturbances necessarily meant trouble that he did not force himself to wakefulness until there was a tap on the door and Jolly asked in a whisper:

'Are you awake, sir?'

'Er—just about,' mumbled Rollison. 'What's the matter? Can't we have some light?' He saw a glow from the other room but Jolly went softly across the bedroom, closed the window and then drew the blackout curtains before

43

returning to the door and switching on the light.

'I'm sorry to disturb you, sir, but nothing I could say would satisfy Mr Grice.'

'Grice?' Rollison exclaimed. 'Here?'

'No, sir. At the Yard. He telephoned and asked if you could go over to see him at once.'

'*Confound* the man!' exclaimed Rollison. 'He would choose the middle of the night. Did he say why?'

'No, sir. And it's nearly seven o'clock. I'll make some tea,' Jolly added hurriedly, 'and a little toast might be acceptable, in case you don't have time to get back for breakfast.'

Jolly closed the door with a snap while Rollison hitched himself up on his pillows, frowned, grew rapidly more curious about the summons from Grice and dressed quickly.

It was cold in the small alcove in spite of an electric fire glowing; the cold spell showed no signs of slackening. Rollison noticed it more because he had climbed out of bed too quickly and had not yet warmed through. Before putting on a collar and tie he shaved and washed in the radiator-heated bathroom.

Jolly had prepared scrambled egg and toast and apologised because the egg was powdered. Rollison nodded, still feeling jaded and conscious of a cold nearer development than it had been the previous night. When he had finished eating he glanced at his watch, then glared at Jolly.

44

'Confound you, it's only a quarter to seven now.'

'Is it, sir?' asked Jolly, concerned. 'Something must be the matter with my watch. I quite thought it was much later. These dark mornings make it so difficult to estimate the time,' he continued glibly. 'Why, it must have been nearly six, not seven, when the Superintendent telephoned.'

'I'll deal with you later,' said Rollison heavily, annoyed with himself because a triviality loomed so large. He lit a cigarette and Jolly reappeared with his greatcoat, hat and gloves: the hat was a different one from that damaged in the canal. Rollison donned the greatcoat gladly and looked forward to walking to the Yard; nothing would warm and freshen him more than that. He nodded to Jolly and went out; Jolly, smiling paternally, closed the door as his footsteps echoed down the stairs.

At the foot of the stairs Rollison paused.

A moroseness and a lack of enthusiasm, greater than the mild deception really deserved, possessed and puzzled him. He felt that something which he had not seen should be obvious, that there was a piece in the puzzle clearly out of place. Indeterminately he stood in the porch and peered into the darkness of the morning. The lights of a milkman's van passed and he heard the rattle of bottles.

Abruptly he snapped his fingers and turned

about.

He re-entered the flat, surprising Jolly at clearing the breakfast-table but too full of the fresh idea to take pleasure out of Jolly's surprise. Stepping to the telephone, he asked:

'What time did Grice call us, Jolly?'

'Well, sir, in view of my error, it must have been in the neighbour-hood of five-forty-five.'

'Call it that,' said Rollison, dialling a number. 'He wasn't at home or at the Yard at half-past eleven, which meant that he wasn't likely to be in bed before one o'clock. More or less,' added the Toff hastily, to prevent argument. 'He went to bed too late to be up and bright soon after five o'clock but must have been up in time to get to the Yard and telephone us when he did.' He explained no more but dialled again, this time getting a response from the Yard. 'Give me Superintendent Grice, please.'

'I don't think he's in yet, sir,' said the operator. 'If you'll hold on a moment I'll find out. Is that Colonel Rollison?'

'That's right,' said Rollison and covered the mouthpiece with his hand. 'Jolly, I remembered only just in time that telephone calls are always open to question. Hallo . . . you're sure he's not in? . . . all right, find out for me whether anyone from the Yard telephoned me about an hour and a quarter ago, will you?' He waited again while Jolly approached and stood silent with obvious

46

concern, until the operator said convincingly: 'No one has called you from here, sir.'

'Right-oh, thanks,' said Rollison and replaced the receiver. As he regarded Jolly there was a fresh light in his eyes and he was no longer conscious of depression or moroseness. 'Jolly, we nearly fell for it. Get a hat and coat and follow me at a reasonable distance.' As he spoke he dialled another number, this time waiting much longer for a reply which came with the sleepy voice of a man just awakened.

'Grice speaking,' announced the voice.

'The last thing in the world I want to do is to disturb you,' Rollison assured the Superintendent with relish, 'but do you use telephones in your sleep?'

Grice grunted and over the line there came creaking noises as he turned over in bed and straightened up. Then he demanded to know what Rollison meant and finally said emphatically that he had not put through a call.

'That's all I want to know,' Rollison assured him. 'Go back to Morpheus and give him my apologies and regrets.'

Jolly, clad in a black overcoat, a muffler and a bowler hat, was waiting when he finished. Rollison lit another cigarette and said lightly:

'Somewhere between here and the Yard things should happen. Keep at least twenty yards away from me but not much farther.

47

'Very good, sir,' said Jolly inadequately.

Rollison's heart was beating fast with excitement as he stepped from the porch of the house and entered Gresham Terrace. This time no milk-van passed and there was silence in the street; no chink of light showed and it was too early for even the faintest trace of dawn. The air was piercingly cold and a keen wind was blowing from the north. Rollison clenched and unclenched his fingers inside his fur-lined gloves to keep them warm and supple. He walked cautiously at first, because of the blackout, but deliberately eschewed a torch for it would betray his presence too easily and, in his mind, there was the possibility of a shot being fired at him out of the blackout. No one would set such a trap without being ready to turn it to full advantage.

His mind roamed. Someone knew of his interest in the affair and wanted him to leave the flat, baiting the trap as a message from Grice. One question raised itself above all others: who knew of his interest?

The Jamesons all knew, of course; and possibly Bimbleton. Beyond that, no one could have an opportunity of knowing and he had little doubt that the news had been circulated through the Jamesons; it was too early to decide how it had been done; there would be time enough to learn that later. One fact did evolve; the 'someone' knew enough about him to fear that his intervention might lead to unwanted hindrances. He remembered how young Jameson had recognised him after a few minutes and knew that many others, familiar with the more sensational stories of crime in the Press, either remembered his photograph or could call it to mind. That was one of the penalties of his earlier enthusiasm, a youthful longing for publicity which had been amply satisfied but had become a disadvantage.

He shrugged the thought aside and continued to walk slowly along the dark streets, turning into Piccadilly and keeping to the buildings opposite Green Park. A few taxis, buses and other vehicles were on the move and the steady tramp of feet came regularly. He heard people hurrying, often the light tap-tap-tap of a woman's heels. His eyes grew accustomed to the darkness and he could see vague shapes a yard or two away from him but recognised none; no one could possibly recognise him.

He wondered whether Jolly was following satisfactorily and, outside the Piccadilly Hotel, paused long enough for the bowler-hatted figure to loom in ghostly silhouette against the insufficient lights of a bus.

'Close up a bit,' said Rollison.

'Very good, sir,' whispered Jolly.

The presence of so many unseen people, the sound of movements divorced from sight of those who were making them and the awareness of the trap which might be sprung at any moment gave an eeriness to the walk which began to play on Rollison's nerves. Near Trafalgar Square he paused again on the pavement of Whitehall and waited for Jolly who appeared rather clearer for the early dawn was lessening the blackness of the eastern sky.

'The one place where I'm sure to go is the Yard,' said Rollison. 'Whatever is coming will happen there.'

'Very likely, sir.'

'Look here,' said Rollison with a touch of irritation, 'I may like an automaton to work for me but I don't like one following me about. Be human. Five yards,' he added and started off again with an echo of 'Very good, sir,' from his man. He smiled wryly at his own touchiness then drew near to the gates of Scotland Yard.

He took off his glove from his right hand and gripped his service revolver inside his greatcoat pocket, keeping his left hand about his torch, still switched off. He reached the gates and grew aware of two dark figures, standing side by side, both wearing steel helmets and blocking his path.

The policemen on duty, of course.

A rustle of movement ahead of him preceded a respectful inquiry: 'Who is that, please?'

'Colonel Rollison,' said Rollison and shone his torch fully into the man's face. The other went back a yard, blinking and surprised, but Rollison recognised the features of a constable whom he had often seen before; the other man was also familiar.

'And a friend,' put in Rollison hastily, to explain Jolly, who had hurried up at the hint of a disturbance. He apologised for his clumsiness with the torch and with Jolly passed between the iron gates. The dark and empty courtyard yawned before him and he said bewilderedly:

'Can anything happen here? Or . . .' He paused and then exclaimed: 'No, confound it! They wanted us out of the flat! I've been too clever. Come on!'

For the first time since leaving Gresham Terrace he hurried, surprising the constables and escaping collision with them only by a hair's breadth. The glowing silhouette of the word 'taxi' in front of a vehicle passing by made him call out and the cab drew into the kerb.

'22G, Gresham Terrace,' said the Toff hurriedly and bundled Jolly in.

He wasted no time in saying what he thought of himself and they sat in silence for ten minutes until they reached the flat in the increasing light of dawn. Rollison jumped out before it stopped moving and hurried into the house and up the stairs, convinced this time that he would make discoveries of importance. The sight of a crack of light beneath the door

51

confirmed this and made him stop abruptly.

Jolly joined him, sedately.

'We've visitors,' whispered the Toff. 'Go to the back door. I'll give you three minutes. Then wait unless I shout for you.'

CHAPTER FIVE

LADY FORLORN

The illuminated dial of his wrist-watch told Rollison when the three minutes had passed. For that time he had waited without making any movement, his ears strained to catch sounds inside the flat. Whoever was there was as careful as he for there was no sound. Once he saw a faint shadow darken the sliver of light but it disappeared quickly. It confirmed that someone was inside and quickened his pulse.

On the tick of three minutes he inserted his key in the lock. It made a faint scratching sound but not one likely to be audible inside. Cautiously he opened the door, as cautiously pushed it wider.

No sound came through.

He stepped over the threshold with his gun in his right hand. His eyes narrowed against the light coming from the lounge which he also used as a study. The small foyer, itself furnished as a lounge where Jolly kept casual callers, was in perfect order except that the drawers of a small bureau were half-open; they had been closed when he had left.

Soft-footed, he crept towards the lounge proper.

The absence of sound was uncanny, unless it meant that he had been heard and the uninvited guest was waiting to strike. Rollison drew near enough to see inside the room then stopped and glared at four easy chairs, their short legs poking towards the ceiling, the light gleaming on the castors. The webbing beneath each chair had been ripped open and the springs revealed in all their nakedness. Against one wall he saw his desk, littered with its contents; the floor was strewn with papers and souvenirs, little things he treasured. Behind it there should have been two etchings in black frames; they had been taken down.

'All in half an hour!' he said inaudibly. 'All right, my fine gentleman.'

Then he heard a movement.

It came from the lounge, a shuffling sound which puzzled and yet made him act swiftly. He pushed the door wider open and covered the room with his gun, saying sharply:

'That's enough!'

Then he peered at what seemed an empty room, chaotic with up-turned chairs and emptied drawers and bureaux. Even the long wall opposite his desk, usually filled with souvenirs of cases in which he had been

53

concerned, was stripped; an assortment of curios was piled on the floor. But despite the movement he saw no one *and there was no other door in the lounge.*

The heavy curtains at the windows were drawn.

Rollison drew a deep breath and stepped farther forward, feeling slightly foolish. As he moved he saw someone behind a chair, someone who appeared to be kneeling. He moved closer to the chair swiftly, to avoid any shot which might be fired from behind it and said again:

'That's enough. Come out.'

Peering over the top of the chair, when there was no response except another faint shuffling movement, he saw a girl. He judged that from the long hair; she was kneeling, or in a similar posture, and he could not see her face. As she made no attempt to look up or to move, Rollison put caution aside and rounded the chair, worried then more than puzzled.

The girl was not kneeling; she was crouching against the open back of the chair and one hand was clutching a spring. Her head lolled forward and about her neck was tied a white scarf. Rollison exclaimed, bent down and raised her to a more comfortable position; relief followed that for the scarf had been used to gag, not strangle, her and her eyes were wide open. She had dark hair, waved slightly and dressed as a page-boy bob; her eyes were enormous, fringed with long dark lashes.

Her feet were tied together and there was a piece of cord about her right wrist; obviously she had freed her wrists and been trying to stand up.

Rollison lifted her to an easy chair and rested her in it. He did not spend time in unfastening the gag or the bonds at her ankles but said quickly:

'I'll be back in two minutes.'

He left the lounge, went into the kitchen and unlocked the back door, whispering:

'Has anything happened there, Jolly?'

'No, sir,' said Jolly softly.

'All right, come in. We've had our birds but they've flown, I think.' He hurried into the living rooms again, switching on the lights of all of them. Three bedrooms were in the same chaotic state as the lounge and the dining room was in no better state. The wardrobes were empty and, after satisfying himself that no one lurked in any corner, Rollison went back to the lounge.

There Jolly had put a couch on its legs and rested the girl on it full-length; he was unfastening her ankles and the gag was removed. The girl was working her mouth to and fro and there were red marks at the corners where the gag had been drawn tightly.

'I'll get you some water,' he said quickly.

'I have a kettle on, sir, for tea,' said Jolly. 'I'll go and make it.'

He finished his work on the bonds at the girl's ankles then left the Toff with her. She was lying with her head on a cushion, staring up at him but not trying to speak. Instead she rubbed the corners of her mouth gingerly with her right hand; about the wrist, beneath the loose cuff of her black silk dress, the flesh was red and puffy except for a white ridge where the cord had been tied.

'I'll do that,' said Rollison and smiled down at her.

As he massaged her lips he appraised her more thoroughly. Her dress and shoes were of good quality and good taste; she wore a single string of pearls and, although it was impossible to be sure without closer inspection, he imagined that they were real, not cultured. She had a three-diamond ring on her engagement finger and the man who had bought it had not been forced to worry about fifty pounds either way; her watch was of diamonds or diamante; if diamonds it was worth a fortune. Her stockings, laddered about her ankles, were of lustreless silk and the slim lines of her ankles made it plain that they had not been so cavalierly treated as her wrists.

After those things, Rollison studied her face.

She had a smooth complexion, the kind which no artifice could contrive in itself but could not be achieved without art. Her nose was rather short, her upper lip also short, the blue of her great eyes a deep, limpid blue. Her hair swept back from a high, broad forehead; but for the redness at her lips she looked perfectly groomed, a picture enough to make most men's hearts beat fast.

Rollison stopped at last and asked quietly:

'Is that better?'

'Ye-es,' said the girl after a pause and then more quickly: 'Yes, oh, thanks so much.' The trite words would have amused him in other circumstances but he saw nothing funny in them then. 'Who are you?' she went on urgently. 'Do you live here?'

'It's my flat,' Rollison assured her.

She glanced away from him and about the room. Then she shifted her position, sitting up against the end of the settee. The expression in her eyes puzzled him but he made no comment and she went on:

'What a foul mess! But—they didn't find it.'

'That's good,' said Rollison heartily. 'What didn't they find?'

'Don't joke, please,' said the girl and glanced towards the door as Jolly entered with a tea tray. He put it down on a table which had not been overturned, bowed and went out; Rollison knew that he would keep within easy hearing distance.

Rollison righted another chair and poured tea, deliberately eyeing the girl as he handed her a cup and she took it with a commendably steady hand.

57

The electric fire made the room so warm that he took off his greatcoat.

'Oh, that's good,' said the girl when the cup was half-finished. Then she said again: 'Who are you?'

'Rollison,' he said. 'Richard Rollison.'

She looked clearly disappointed.

'I haven't heard of you,' she told him. 'I thought you'd be Peveril, but—' She broke off abruptly and took another sip of tea while Rollison asked:

'Who is Peveril?'

The girl finished drinking, put her cup down and returned his gaze evenly.

'I don't really know but I've heard him mentioned. He—don't you know him?'

'Not yet,' said Rollison.

He found it difficult not to laugh at her expression; it was bewildered and just a little irritated. That in itself would not have been enough for laughter but the general situation, with all its inherent absurdities, struck him as comic. Thought of the long walk through the blackout expecting an attack to develop at any moment, while the flat was being ransacked and the girl left there, had its own peculiar humours. He repeated gravely:

'Not yet but there's time and I've a number of things that need clearing up. How are you feeling?' He glanced at her long and shapely legs and added: 'Can you walk, do you think?'

'I—I expect so.' She put her feet to the floor

58

and he helped her to stand. She was a little unsteady but did not fall or lean upon him too heavily. She was tall, the top of her head on a line with his eyes. 'Yes, I'm all right. I wish—I wish I knew what to say. You *aren't* Peveril?' When he shook his head she shrugged and added: 'I was sure that was where they were coming, they were sure Peveril had it last night. I heard them talking, there isn't any doubt about it.'

'Of course not,' said Rollison drily. 'There's no doubt about it at all. After all, it must be about somewhere.' His eyes were smiling at her and for a moment she eyed him uncertainly, sober-faced and not catching his mood. Then she realised that he was laughing at her and her expression changed; the slightest upwards curve of her reddened lips brought a dimple in either cheek and her eyes held a gleam.

But she still sounded puzzled.

'Don't you know anything about it?'

'I know that someone telephoned me to get me out of the flat and visited it while I was gone,' said Rollison. That—and no more and it isn't a great deal. Given time it will work itself out, I suppose.' He pulled a chair towards her and grimaced when she sank low into it because of the damaged webbing. Sitting on the arm of another, he commented: 'They forgot that it might have been hidden in the arms, didn't they?'

'No,' said the girl. 'They heard your taxi and hurried out the back way before you came. They were just going to start on the arms.'

'Oh,' said Rollison blankly. Then tentatively: 'You heard them say that, too, of course.'

'Yes, I—oh, you fool!' She smiled more widely and there was a measure of relief in her manner. 'This isn't half as bad as I thought it was going to be,' she said. 'I'd imagined Peveril coming in and shouting and bellowing right and left.'

Rollison put his head on one side.

'You don't know Peveril but you know his temperament?' She frowned a little.

'Yes, I've heard about it.'

She stopped abruptly for Rollison was chuckling and making no attempt to hide it. After a moment, she joined him. By then the constraint between them had quite disappeared and as Rollison leaned forward and poured out more tea he took his cigarette case from his pocket and proffered it. Smoking, he said:

'Now tell me all about it, Miss—'!

'Lancing. June Lancing.'

'Thanks,' said Rollison. '*Richard* Rollison.'

She laughed again; it was easy to see that she had not suffered much more than inconvenience and her experience did not weigh heavily upon her. He even wondered whether it weighed too lightly and if she had

60

been left at the flat with the sole purpose of confusing him. He did not set the thought aside, nor did he brood upon it. 'Now let's get started,' he said. 'It's going to be easier for you to start at the beginning and tell the story, isn't it? I hope you will. I've some right to know what it's about, even though I'm not Peveril.' He streamed smoke towards the ceiling as he waited for her reaction, seeing her frown with indecision and then nod abruptly.

'Yes, you have, but—well, I was going to advise you to have nothing to do with it but if they searched your flat you must be involved somewhere, mustn't you?'

He did not answer and she went on with sudden excitement:

'Unless they came to the wrong flat. Do you think that's happened?'

'No,' said Rollison with emphasis. 'They took too much trouble getting me out and they knew both mine and my servant's name.'

'Oh,' said June. 'That rather spoils the idea. I—I hardly know where to start but I'll do my best.'

'Supposing we start with the "it"?' asked Rollison. 'What is it?'

She eyed him blankly.

'*I* don't know. I only know they're looking for it and thought Peveril had it. But as they came here they must think that you know where it is. When I say I don't know,' she added hastily, 'I mean that I'm not sure what's

61

in it, in fact I haven't any idea. It's a black case, something like a jewel case. I've only seen it once and I didn't look inside. There's rather a queer story attached to it.'

'Rather queer!' exclaimed Rollison. 'You beat the band on understatements! But we aren't making a lot of progress and I have to be at the office before long. Can you give me just the essentials?' He was no more interested in going to the office than he was with the eight o'clock news, which he had missed for the first time in weeks, but spoke casually to try to get her started. He had not yet tried to reconcile the visit and the guest who could not help herself with the affair of Jameson but it had not occurred to him that they were unconnected.

'It really begins before I had the black case. My fiancé's father owned it and whatever is in it. He sent for me a week or two ago and acted rather strangely.' She paused and then lost herself in her story; Rollison could almost see her trying to read reason into what had happened while she talked. 'He seemed rather scared, as if something might happen to him, and talked rather morbidly. Lionel's out East and he said he didn't think he would ever see his son again—you know the way oldish people do get, sometimes, don't they?' Rollison said that he did. He did not add that either June Lancing's attitude towards 'oldish people' had more than the avenge heedlessness of youth, or else she had no great regard for her future father-in-law.

'Well, he gave me the case and asked me to make sure that Lionel had it as soon as he returned to the country—if he did return, he had to say that. If not, I could open it myself and there would be directions inside saying what to do with it. I was tempted to look inside,' confessed June frankly. 'I thought once it might be some family jewel but I was so busy at the time that I didn't get beyond being tempted.' She smoothed her hair back and the electric light gleamed on the fire of the three diamonds of her ring. 'I just locked it in a drawer in my dressing-table. Then the old man—I mean Mr Brett, Lionel's father—went abroad; he's in the rubber business and was going to America for consultations on synthetic rubber, I think—and for a couple of days I practically forgot about it. It would still be locked in the drawer if—if it hadn't been stolen.'

She meant, of course, that she had successfully overcome a temptation to investigate; it was easy to imagine that when she had reached a decision she would stick to it.

'I thought it was an ordinary burglar. It was at night and I was lying down for an hour—I was on fire-watch duty and didn't get undressed. The man came in the room and started searching and my heart was beating nineteen to the dozen. Then he found the locked drawer and took out the case. Most of my jewels were in the drawer but he didn't worry about them. He put the case in his pocket and went out. So I—I followed him.'

'Unobserved?' queried the Toff.

'I suppose so. He didn't seem to notice me. I live in a block of flats at Putney,' the girl explained, 'and he only went up the next flight and into a flat there. Later I heard them talking; there's an empty flat next to theirs and the walls have been cracked by bomb-blast—they don't know that. I heard them talking about Peveril and what kind of man he is. Apparently the case was stolen from them and they thought Peveril had it. I had to go to the office and couldn't follow them all the time but I kept watching the flat and tonight—I mean last night—I heard them planning to make another effort to get the case. I followed them,' she said simply, 'and we got here about four o'clock in the morning. They waited outside—it was freezing cold but I stuck it out somehow.' She smiled a little vaguely. 'Then I followed them up the stairs. I thought I wasn't seen but one of them turned round and waited for me. I couldn't even shout or put up a fight,' she added ruefully. 'They gagged and bound me and pushed me behind the chair; I heard them talking as they worked, as I've told you. Then one of them outside came in and said you were here, so they went out the back way.

I was trying to get my hands free when you came,' she finished simply. 'That's all there is in it as far as I can tell you. Except the frills and you asked me not to take too long.'

'I did,' admitted Rollison thoughtfully. A pause and then: 'As a story it's as plausible as any I've heard but it doesn't ring all the bells.'

'What do you mean?' she demanded.

'Item one: Why didn't you go to the police? They're quite used to dealing with burglars. Why did you take on the whole party by yourself?' Rollison leaned back as he spoke but his expression left no doubt as to his meaning and for the first time the girl's cheeks flushed hotly.

'Put yourself in my position and ask yourself whether you'd believe such a story, 'said Rollison. 'Now, supposing we have the real truth?'

CHAPTER SIX

'WHAT'S IN A NAME?'

June Lancing rose sharply from her chair but stumbled, still stiff from her bonds. Her eyes were bright with anger, her hands were clenched, her attitude was one of belligerent hostility. She eyed the Toff without trying to hide her anger; but that emotion might well be feigned and in any case Rollison did not find it disturbing.

'Before you get hot-headed, do as I say and put yourself in my position,' he advised equably. 'Well?'

'You're impertinent! I've told you what happened.'

'Possibly,' conceded the Toff, 'but you haven't justified your actions.'

'Do I need to? To you?'

'Well, out of gratitude you might,' murmured Rollison. 'Out of necessity you will; because if you don't tell me the police will be interviewing you within thirty minutes and I don't think you want to talk to the police now any more than you did when you elected to follow the thieves on your own. All normal and good-living citizens always go the police in times of trouble,' he added lightly. 'Even the most adventurous spirits don't try more than once to investigate on their own. It's an English characteristic,' he added, 'and it's surprising how we run true to form. When we don't we become suspect and therefore I suspect you.'

'Don't be small-minded! I've told you the truth, and—' She paused. 'Are you serious about going to the police? No, you can't be. Why should you?'

Rollison put his head on one side and regarded her in marvelling silence for some seconds. Then with an expressive gesture he

66

indicated the state of the room and murmured:

'Another English characteristic is to go to the police when they have the kind of visitor I had today. There are exceptions,' he added cautiously, 'and provided I'm convinced that it's necessary I could be one. Although there's the matter of insurance, the company will want police testimony that the damage was done by thieves before they'll repair it free of charge. The damage isn't negligible,' he added mildly.

'Oh, damage. That's what's worrying you.' She was contemptuous. 'Send the bill in to me. I'll pay it.'

'Well, well!' exclaimed Rollison. 'The girl with the answer to everything. Now, do try to get this clear. People don't do unreasonable things without a strong motive and your attitude is unreasonable. What's the motive?' He stood up and leaned against the mantelpiece, gazing down on her and appreciating the contours of her face and the agitated rise and fall of her breasts. He thought she would shout at him to do what he liked but she said tensely:

'I daren't go to the police.'

'Daren't is frank enough, anyhow,' conceded Rollison.

'I'm being frank about everything. I—I'm not English. I'm an alien and I've no right in the country without registering with the police. I haven't done so. Does that satisfy you?' she added waspishly and then turned her head away, hiding the expression in her eyes but not before he had seen the hint of fear in them.

As she spoke he remembered Grice's harassed comment: 'Aliens, aliens, nothing but aliens.' But her statement surprised him; she had no accent and if her appearance was not typically English he knew a dozen English 'types' who varied at least as much as she from the popular conception of blue eyes and golden hair. She was worried, though, and trying hard not to break down and implore him to keep away from the police; in her there was a pride which might one day fall but would sustain her through most eventualities.

'June Lancing sounds English,' he said quietly.

'It's an assumed name. At least,' she corrected, 'partly assumed. My mother's maiden name was Lancing; she was English.'

'That would help with the police and friendly aliens—'

She lifted a hand, long and tapering, the white palm turned towards him.

'I'm not a "friendly" alien. She sneered the 'friendly.' My father was a Rumanian.'

'There are even enemy aliens as free as the air,' said Rollison mildly.

'That's the way an Englishman would talk,' she stormed at him. 'You don't know anything about what happens in your own country! If I were to be detained now and examined, it would take weeks before the authorities were satisfied with my *bona fides*, even though I was brought up in England and have spent years over here. Weeks? Months, more likely! Oh, they would treat me all right but they'd pen me up with hundreds of others until everything was "in order" and I can't afford to be interned even for a few weeks. I've too much to do.' She hesitated, then dropped her hands in a helpless gesture. 'But you'll do your duty like any stiff-necked officer and gentleman. I know your type.'

She turned and stood with her back towards him.

Rollison contemplated a wisp of hair at the back of her head; it was out of place, a faint blemish on the smooth, dark sheen. He pursed his lips and allowed the silence to be prolonged; a clock in the dining-room struck half-past eight. It was a signal for her to turn and her expression was dejected, her eyes tearful.

Slowly and sadly Rollison shook his head.

'No, I'm not so soft-hearted,' he said drily. 'I've seen too many women pretending to cry. If I delay telling the police it won't be because of the appeal in your lovely eyes, so you needn't keep it up.'

Anger burned afresh in her eyes.

'You pig! You—'

'If I keep away from them *pro tem* it will be because I think whatever job you're doing

69

warrants it,' continued Rollison, 'and then not till I'm convinced that you've told me the truth and not pitched a beautiful fairy story. But we won't argue about that now. I'll let you stay here until I am satisfied and I'll give you fair warning of what I'm going to do. That will have to be enough for the time being. Now— do you want to alter anything you've told me? This is the best chance you'll have.'

'You know the truth,' she said stiffly.

'Did your fiancé's father know your nationality?'

'He did not.'

'Your fiancé?'

'Yes,' she said abruptly. 'I've told him and he agreed that I ought to say nothing about it. No one suspects me of being Rumanian and my work—'

'We'll talk about the work later,' said Rollison. 'You're quite sure that you don't know what's in the little black case?'

'I've no idea at all.'

'How many men were in the flat of the man who stole it?'

'I don't know,' said June sharply. 'Four or five, anyhow. I heard at least four different voices.'

'Did you hear any names?'

'Oh, what do names matter? I wasn't worrying about names.'

'Everything considered, you weren't worrying about enough,' said Rollison tartly.

'The names are important. Do you remember any?' She drew a deep breath.

'I know one was called Smith.' She uttered that challengingly, as if conscious of the fact that such a name might sound a deliberate fake. 'There was another peculiar one, I don't really remember it. Something like "gibbet" and the others called him 'Ibby' more often than anything else. I don't remember the others, I'm not even sure that any others were used. I—' She broke off and stared at him in astonishment. 'What on earth's the matter with you?'

'The matter,' breathed the Toff. 'Nothing's the matter, my sweet, except that you've really said something worthwhile. The name was Ibbetson, wasn't it?'

'Ibbetson! That's it.'

'And Ibbetson is the missing link, although he might not like to know it,' said Rollison very softly. He felt as elated as he looked, standing up and thrusting his hands deep in his pockets as he regarded her. 'I think I shall probably be glad that you came, after all. Was "Jameson" mentioned?'

'I don't remember it,' said June.

'What about "Tom"?'

'There wasn't anyone called Tom,' she assured him. 'I would remember a short name like that. But—look here, I must be going, I can't stay away from the office this morning, we're absolutely rushed off our feet. I

71

promised to be there by eight o'clock.'

'I think you'll have to pretend a headache,' said Rollison, regretfully, 'and wait for a while.' Before she interrupted he went on: 'I'll telephone a message for you, if you like. Where do you perform the slavery?' He did not add: 'Why do you need to work if you can so casually offer to pay for the damage here?' but waited for her quick, sharp response.

'At the Gower Street Red Cross Depot. I— oh, I don't see why I should *beg* you to let me go but there's a big consignment of mail in from German prison camps and another due in from the Far East today and one from Italy expected any time. We can't let them accumulate; it's too cruel to keep relatives waiting for mail a minute more than necessary.'

There was no faking; she was sincere, her plea was heartfelt; its genuine ring was not one which could be forced. For the first time he was tempted to let her go but he steadied himself, for she might be lying so easily.

'*Will* you let me go?' she demanded.

'Just a moment,' said Rollison. 'Are you understaffed at Gower Street?'

'Of course we are!'

'Are there men as well as women working there?'

'What difference does that make?'

'Are there?' persisted Rollison.

'Yes, but—'

72

'Then you can go,' said Rollison, very amiably, 'and you have a voluntary helper for the day. Or nearly voluntary,' he added. 'Jolly. Jolly!'

'Coming, sir,' said Jolly. He appeared promptly, his mournful face showing little expression. 'Can I do anything, sir?'

'You can join the Red Cross as a temporary helper in Miss Lancing's office,' said Rollison lightly. 'Work diligently and go with Miss Lancing to the office, to lunch and escort her back here when you've finished.' He looked at the girl, whose chin was thrust forward but who made no objection and added to her: 'That's the one condition. Will you keep it?'

'Oh, I'll fit him in somewhere,' said June disparagingly. 'He'll be helplessly slow, it needs practice but—' She stopped abruptly and surprised Rollison by the sudden warmth of her expression and her eyes. 'But I'm being a beast; it's really generous of you. Of course, he'll be invaluable.'

'Thank you, miss,' said Jolly. His eyes were pained as he regarded Rollison's uncompromising face. 'If you really require it, sir, I will get my hat and coat. I was about to prepare breakfast but—'

'I haven't time to eat,' said June.

Five minutes later Rollison watched them walking along the street, the girl hurrying, clad in a mink coat which had been in one corner of the lounge and making Jolly lengthen his normal sedate stride. The sight of the precise, black-clad servant and the hatless, eager girl amused Rollison and yet his smile was tinged with uncertainty. Then it grew set, for he saw a man walk in the wake of the couple, a man who had been walking much more slowly a few seconds before.

'This is going to be another unpopular day for me at the office,' he said, *sotto voce*.

Grabbing his greatcoat he hurried out of the door with one arm in a sleeve and the other pulling the door to. Although he saw the man who sprang from the shadows of the landing, he could do nothing to save himself from a heavy blow on the side of the head which half-stunned him and sent him pitching forward. He banged his head again when he struck the floor and lost consciousness after another blow on the left temple. He had a momentary image of his attacker, short, dark clad, with an arm up raised, before everything faded.

CHAPTER SEVEN

IBBY ON THE JOB

The thick-set assailant wasted no time in looking at the Toff but bent down and unceremoniously dragged him back into the flat, feet first. He returned to the passage and pulled the door to, waiting and listening. No doors opened below and there was no indication that the tenants of the other flats had been disturbed. The man went down the first flight of stairs to a landing window and glanced out. He raised his thumb and was seen by a man walking on the far side of the street. In a few seconds the second man had joined the first and in a space of three minutes two others also arrived.

Then the flat door was closed and locked.

Amongst the company was a small, plump man, dressed neatly in light grey. His cheeks were rosy and shining, his blue eyes smiled and he gave the impression of being in the best of good tempers. Removing a velour hat he ran a pink palm over dark hair lined with grey and said in a soft, persuasive voice:

'Now boys, let's get along with it; we haven't a lot of time. Ibby's on the job, remember, and we mustn't fall down on it. What didn't we do?'

The thick-set man said:

'We were going to start on the arms of the chairs.'

'That's right, so we were.' There was the faintest of lisps in Ibbetson's voice. 'Charley, you and Mike go into the dining-room; Fred and me will do the lounge.' He sent the other couple into the farther room, large men, although neither of them would have been noticed in a crowd, and glanced down at Rollison. 'We'd better take him with us, Fred.'

The thick-set man grunted and together they lifted the Toff and carried him to the settee where June Lancing had rested not long before. His head lolled backwards unnaturally and his lips were slightly open.

'What a cinch,' said Ibbetson, with a gentle chuckle. 'I thought he was going to cause trouble but you never can tell. Now let's get on with it, Fred.'

'I'm waiting for you,' declared the Toff's assailant gruffly.

Using knives which ripped through the tapestry covering of the armchairs, they stripped the arms down to the springs and searched inside. Neither of them talked while they were working and there was no sound from the other room. The chairs finished, Ibbetson's plump face and red lips set in vexation but, beyond uttering a mild expletive, he made no comment. Together they shifted the furniture to one end of the room and

76

rolled back a colourful Mirzapore carpet; the floor boards revealed no hiding-place, even when they moved the furniture again and tried the other end.

Ibbetson bit his lips and went to join the others. They shook their heads at his soft-voiced question.

'It must be somewhere.' said Ibbetson. 'He wouldn't have kept it in his pocket, would he?' He hurried to Rollison and searched him thoroughly but found nothing of interest except his revolver, which was removed. That finished, he went to each room, surveyed it carefully and nodded after a few seconds, as if deciding that nothing had been overlooked. Something under an hour after they had arrived the quartet gathered in the lounge and Ibbetson sat on an upturned chair.

'We'll have to make him talk,' he declared roundly.

'What, here?' demanded Fred.

'Yes, of course; we can't take him through the streets of London like that, Fred. Where's your common sense?' The mild reproof administered, Ibbetson leaned forward and looked at the Toff whose head rested more naturally on the end of the settee, close to a spring which jutted though the covering and the webbing and canvas beneath. 'He looks bad, Fred; you didn't hit him *too* hard, did you? I wouldn't like to think he wouldn't come round.'

'He'll come round,' growled the thick-set man. 'Fetch a jug o' water, one of you.'

Lying quite comfortably and with nothing the matter with him beyond an ache at either temple, the Toff heard the injunction, as he had heard everything which Ibbetson and the others had said since the gathering in the lounge; he had regained consciousness while the settee had been shifted for a second time and without opening his eyes had guessed what the others were doing. That the men had stayed within easy distance in order to finish their job did not surprise him; what angered him was that he had not thought of the possibility. The man who had started to follow Jolly and June Lancing had been a bait, just as the telephone call had been; and it had proved equally effective.

The prospect of being doused with a jug of water did not appeal to him; on the other hand, the cold water would be refreshing and by then the room was uncomfortably warm; the searchers had not switched off the electric fire. He stayed there without moving while soft footsteps sounded in the flat and then, abruptly and without warning, icy water splashed over his face.

He started and even opened his eyes; the impact came with such a surprise that he could not help himself. He recovered quickly, grunted and then settled his head down again. Through narrowed eyes he saw a man in light

78

grey peering down at him; the next moment his head was pushed to one side as the man slapped him sharply across the face; there was no playfulness in the slap.

The Toff's eyes widened.

'That's better, that's better,' said Ibbetson. His soft, lisping voice and plump face were at variance with the viciousness of the blow while in his voice there crept a note of harshness which alone told the Toff that it would be unwise to judge from appearances where the plump man was concerned. 'Keep them open, Rollison, or you'll get—another!'

A second slap, on the other cheek, pushed Rollison's head to the opposite side.

'That's just a little warning,' said Ibbetson softly. 'Don't sing out or make a noise or you'll get a lot worse. And we won't leave you here alive; we don't like leaving men who can talk. Pull him up, Fred.'

Fred revealed surprising strength; he gripped Rollison's lapels with one hand and pulled him to a sitting position. With his other hand he swept Rollison's legs from the settee so that the victim was sitting normally, his cheeks flushed and his eyes a little bloodshot but otherwise looking quite normal.

'We don't want any misunderstanding,' said Ibbetson in the same deceptively mild tones. 'We want the box, that's all. Just tell us where the box is and you'll be all right. We don't mean any harm to you personally, unless you get in our way. Now, that's clear enough, and don't—*argue!*'

He shot out his right hand for a third slap.

The Toff moved his head back so smartly that he felt a crick in the neck; but he had the satisfaction of seeing Ibbetson stagger forward when his blow missed and fall on to him. The Toff felt no qualms about raising his right knee and catching the man in the pit of the stomach. A gasp of sheer anguish followed Ibbetson's exclamation of surprise at missing his blow. He sprawled downwards over Rollison who put both hands against the man's chest and thrust him backwards. Ibbetson staggered until Fred stopped his retreat; he would have slumped to the floor had the thick-set man failed to support him.

The other two stared at Rollison, momentarily so startled that they were inactive. The blow and counter-blow had happened so quickly that Ibbetson's hand might still have been moving through the air.

Rollison knew that what chance he had of escaping without injury depended on his speed of action then but was not sure that he could trust his legs. He put them to the test, getting up in one movement. His right knee bent beneath him. He regained his balance and flung himself towards the kitchen door. The man named Charley shot out a hand to stop him but clutched only the sleeve of his coat. Rollison pulled it away. Only Mike stood between the Toff and the door; if he reached it he would surely get through. He swung his left arm, hoping to catch the man and send him off his balance; but Mike evaded it as easily as Rollison had evaded Ibbetson's slap and pushed out his right foot.

The Toff fell over it.

The thud of the crash shook the pictures which remained on the walls, set glasses and vases quivering and the bared springs humming and twanging. It knocked the breath out of Rollison's body and at the same moment a knee forced itself into the small of his back, stout fingers clutched his right wrist and twisted his arm in a hammer lock so excruciating that he bit his lips to prevent himself from crying out in pain. Mike muttered harsh obscenities into his ear and increased the pressure until sweat gathered in globules on his forehead and a vein rose out in his neck, the blood beating fast through it. He did not think that he could stand more of it without fainting and there was a red mist in front of his eyes, a loud drumming in his ears.

Through the drumming words forced themselves but he did not hear Ibbetson say harshly:

'Go easy, Mike, we want the —d alive,'

The pain and pressure alike relaxed. Rollison went down on his face, turning his cheek to the carpet and gasped for breath. He felt the blood rushing to his head and was

81

incapable of thinking, even of feeling afraid. Not until he was hauled to his feet and pushed into an easy chair did his head clear a little; even then he could not see the four men clearly; their figures swayed and danced in front of his eyes.

'Give him some water to drink,' said Ibbetson.

One man held his head back, the other forced a little water between his lips. He choked on it but swallowed enough to refresh him. With that came the knowledge that he was being given a rough-and-ready first-aid so that he might be a better subject for questioning. Now that it was over he realised what a fool he had been to make the attempt; before he might have bluffed his way out, now they would wreak vengeance for its own sake. As his vision steadied he saw the plump face of Ibbetson, livid with rage; Ibbetson was still crouching forward a little to ease his discomfort.

'You've asked for it,' he said softly. 'You're going to get it. But, before that, where's the box?'

Facts began to register on Rollison's mind, obvious ones, although they had been vague and half-formed until that moment. Primarily, they wanted the box about which June Lancing had told him; above everything else they wanted it and they put its possession above the simple matter of revenge for his violence.

They were convinced that he had it or knew where it was; unless that were so, they would not have made the exhaustive search of the flat.

There *must* be a way to force them to wait and hold their hand.

'*The box*,' said Ibbetson. He pushed his face close to Rollison's, keeping it not six inches away. His eyes were smaller, his sandy lashes sparse and coarse. '*Where's the box?*' he whispered and as the question was repeated someone Rollison could not see gripped his wrist and began to force it back. '*The box*,' repeated Ibbetson hoarsely. 'We're going to get it.'

Rollison said with an effort:

'You won't get it this way.'

'Oh, we won't, won't we? Back a bit farther, Mike; we'll teach the runt.' Mike obeyed and the pressure at Rollison's wrist increased, grew as excruciating as the hammer-lock. Perspiration gathered again and he felt the pulse beating in his neck but forced his voice to keep steady.

'I can get it—in person,' he said. He had to fight to keep his eyes wide open: Ibbetson's pupils seemed to get larger every moment.

'Ease off a minute, Mike,' said Ibbetson, after a pause. '*What's* that you said? No tricks now, no tricks.'

The easing of the pressure caused a pain so great that Rollison gasped; then relief flowed through the wrist and he contrived to answer.

'I said that I can get it in person.'

'And what about sending a messenger,' demanded Ibbetson, in the same soft menacing tone. 'What about signing a little note saying I can get it for you? Where is it?' he snapped.

'If anyone gets it, I will,' said Rollison.

They stared at each other for what seemed an age; Rollison's eyes matched Ibbetson's, who was trying to out-stare him and wear down his resistance; with the pain at his wrist again, Rollison knew that he might falter and confess that he was lying, begin the trail of denials that would get him nowhere. But suddenly Ibbetson blinked and stood back a foot; the movement eased the strain at Rollison's eyes and he lowered them without completely closing them.

'You'll get it, all right, because I want it,' said Ibbetson. 'Come on, where is it?'

'I've said all I'm going to until your ape releases my wrist and I've had a rest,' said Rollison thickly. 'You damned fool, do you think I'd put that where anyone can walk in and get it? If I don't collect it myself, it won't be collected.'

'So that's your angle,' said Ibbetson softly. 'Let his wrist go, Mike, we don't want to hurt the poor fellow.' Rollison felt all pressure go from his wrist and hitched himself more comfortably in the chair. The few moments of respite were precious but, having gained them, he could see no way of turning them to full advantage. If he knew what was in the box, if he could talk on terms with the men, he might make progress. As it was he assumed the contents were of immense value and talked as if he knew that and also just why it was wanted.

Ibbetson backed farther away.

'Listen to me, Rollison.' His voice grew stronger. 'Maybe you don't think I'm serious but there's no kidding. There's four of us here and we can kill you a lot of different ways. We don't want to but we can, see—show him your gun, Fred.' The stocky man took an automatic from his pocket and kept it in his hand. 'Show him your knife, Charley.' One of the others slid a clasp-knife from his belt, opened a blade and whetted his thumb on it; it looked razor sharp. That's just two ways,' said Ibbetson. 'No one knows we're here and no one will know who croaked you, Rollison. If you don't show me the way I'm going to get that case, we've got to use some way or other of finishing you, see? The case is important but maybe you're working that angle too much. It's not so important as us getting away and we aren't staying more than another five minutes. Now, open up and no kidding.'

CHAPTER EIGHT

NO KIDDING

In the immediate past, minutes had been of vital importance, now seconds counted almost as much. Rollison eyed the little plump man, trying to estimate his chances of a further bluff and thinking desperately. Had he possessed the case he might have deposited it with his bank, or in a safe deposit at his office.

At his office, in the heart of Whitehall. He felt a spasm of relief and gratitude for the idea, straightened his shoulders and said slowly:

'It's at my office.'

'You heard me say no kidding,' returned Ibbetson. 'Soldiers don't have offices. If you think you can—'

'I'm not thinking anything,' snapped Rollison. 'I've a staff appointment at Whitehall and I've put the case in my office safe. No one can get in the building without a pass and no one can open the safe without a chit from me.'

Ibbetson's eyes narrowed.

'Say, that's smart,' he admitted. 'That's smart, Rollison, but it's tough on you. If we can't get it out it's no use chin-wagging with you, is it? Your knife won't make so much noise as a gun, Charley, make it quick.'

He waved a hand, urging Charley forward.

Rollison did not turn his eyes towards the knife but spoke quietly to Ibbetson.

'Put your head in a noose, if you want to.' He paused, seeing the man's eyes narrow a fraction, not certain whether Ibbetson was really proposing to do murder or whether it was a further stage in the interrogation; he leaned towards the latter theory but the four men were crowding too close, the knife was too sharp, for him to feel any confidence. 'You might get away from here without me and without having the police after you but it isn't likely.'

'What's he say?' demanded one of the men.

'Doesn't he understand plain English?' asked Rollison, with every appearance of contempt.

'He understands *plain* English,' breathed Ibbetson softly. 'But he doesn't get you. Nor do I, Rollison. You're forgetting what I told you—no kidding.'

Rollison shrugged. He was feeling easier at the wrist and arm but his head was throbbing and his eyes felt hot and prickly; little grains of sand seemed to be beneath the lids. He was in no shape to make another attempt to force his way out and he wished he felt more capable of outwitting Ibbetson.

He did not answer immediately and Charley made an impatient movement with the knife; on Rollison the conviction that they were prepared to kill was growing. It made his heart beat fast and his mouth feel dry.

'Open up, *Mister* Rollison,' said Ibbetson.

Rollison said: 'I'm trying to find the short words you can't fail to understand. You know that I work with Grice.'

'So what?' asked Ibbetson.

'Grice is a nice fellow but he doesn't always trust me,' said Rollison. 'He thinks I might put something across him. He doesn't know about the box, for instance, and he doesn't know whom I'm contacting. So he has me watched.'

One of the quartet drew in a sharp breath.

'If this were after dark he couldn't do much,' said Rollison, 'but he'll see you go and he'll have accurate descriptions of you. If the police come here and find me dead, they won't be long putting the descriptions out.'

Another man breathed sharply inwards.

'Go on, go on,' urged Ibbetson. 'You can talk, I'll grant you that. But be careful, no—'

'I know, no kidding,' said Rollison testily and then burst out as if his temper was getting beyond control, although he felt cooler than at any time since they had arrived; he had them guessing. 'Do you think I want that knife in my ribs? I'm in a spot and I know it. You're in one, too, but you don't realise it. If I leave here with you the police might notice you and send a report but they won't know why you came. And if I get to the office with you, I can take you up to the safe. You certainly can't get in

88

the building without me.'

'So you're going to be a guide for the tour, are you?' sneered Ibbetson. 'I don't think! If we let you out of here you'll run yelling for the dicks.' He moved forward so suddenly that Rollison was taken by surprise and put his hands about Rollison's throat. The pressure was tight and firm and Rollison gasped for breath. The man's eyes grew larger, the pupils seemed to be distending as he stared. Rollison's breathing grew laboured and there was a constricting band about his chest.

For that one moment he thought that the man was calling his bluff but then the pressure relaxed and Ibbetson said harshly:

'Take a load of this, Rollison. You'll bring that box here at twelve o'clock. Twelve o'clock on the dot. You'll be watched all the time and if you don't hand the box over to my man waiting here, if you have the police on your tail or try to pull any fast ones, you'll be shot up. I'm not fooling; this is more than a game to me.' He released Rollison and pushed him backwards and then motioned his head towards the door. 'Out, boys,' he said. 'I'll watch him.'

One by one they left the flat.

Rollison watched them, breathing heavily and finding it hard to believe that they were really withdrawing. Mike, Charley and Fred left and he saw each of them step through the door to the landing. Ibbetson waited until they had gone and the front door was pulled to but not closed. Not once did he remove his gaze from Rollison's; he seemed to be trying to hypnotise his victim.

'You heard me,' he said at last. 'No tricks. Twelve on the dot or you'll be shot up. And if you see that skirt, tell her to keep her nose out of this business or she'll get what she doesn't like.'

'That's clear enough,' said Rollison thinly.

'Don't forget it,' said Ibbetson. 'Don't forget any of it.'

He backed to the door and went out quickly; Rollison heard him turning the key in the lock.

Rollison made no effort to move, not even as far as the window. A cold sweat of relief damped his forehead and the nape of his neck and he found breathing difficult. For a long time he stared at the door, expecting it to open again and Ibbetson to reappear—or Charley, with the knife.

It was a bad five minutes but it dragged by without incident and although he heard no further sound, he felt sure that Ibbetson had gone.

'No kidding,' breathed the Toff and rose unsteadily and went to the door.

It took him five minutes to pick the lock, although in his key case there was a skeleton key in the use of which he was no tyro. By the time the door was open his hands were steadier and he felt much better when he went into the bathroom and washed first in hot and then in cold water. After that he went into the kitchen and began to run cold water into the kettle. Abruptly he stopped, turned off the tap and went to the dining-alcove. From a cabinet he took whisky and soda, mixed himself a moderate drink and drank it in two gulps.

He glanced at his watch; it was twenty-five past nine. There was little he could do amidst the chaos of the flat and he found it difficult to decide on his best course of action. He should see Grice, he should be in the office, he should make some plans for midday. The nightmare of the past hour was receding slowly but its effect was still sobering even though, in retrospect, the fears of Charley's knife faded and it was hard to believe that murder had been contemplated.

'Unless,' he said slowly, 'unless Ibbetson really thinks he's a big shot, above the law. Can the little swab think that?'

After another five minutes, while he tried foolishly to straighten the furniture and stopped to contemplate the confusion ruefully, he felt much better. He found that the beds had been ripped open to the springs and that the kitchen was also untidy; the door of the frigidaire was standing open; they had even looked there for the case, the little black case he had never seen and with which "June Lancing's" prospective father-in-law had entrusted her. What was the man's name? Brett, yes, Brett; he was something to do with big business and was on his way to America for discussions. He had a son named Lionel in the Army in the East.

'And two and two make four,' said Rollison aloud. 'I must get a hold on myself. I'm going to pieces. Brett, father and son, might know something more than June does. Then there's the temperamental Mr Peveril whom she thought might live here.' He rubbed the back of his head and eyed the whisky bottle thoughtfully. 'And the box or case is connected with Ibbetson who was the owner of the car which the crazy Commando used after his murder mania. Everything ties up somewhere but I don't remember being more rattled than I am now.'

That confession off his mind, he straightened his clothes and rubbed some embrocation into his right wrist. His elbow was sore from the hammer-lock but he could not get at it effectively and he postponed treatment. Straightening his tie in front of the bathroom mirror, he confided:

'The office first, I think; they'll certainly watch me go. There's nothing I can do about this mess until Jolly gets back.'

Five minutes later, at a quarter to ten, he left the flat and walked slowly towards Piccadilly. He did not appear to be followed but did not believe that he was unobserved. He made no effort to evade pursuit but continued his walk to Whitehall and was later acknowledged cheerfully by the guards at the doors of the big building and the commissionaire inside. Several members of the staff who knew him exchanged breezy greetings and there was a general buzz of excitement, even elation, which puzzled him. Although it was his rule to be at the office by a quarter to nine and he expected some evidence of disgruntlement amongst the staff, he was received with wide smiles and gay good mornings; the girls looked fresh and pretty, if business-like, in khaki blouses and skirts.

Comparison with them made him feel more jaded.

'Good morning,' he said gruffly. 'Is there any post in yet?'

'Very little, sir,' the senior girl told him. 'Isn't it wonderful?'

'Is it?' demanded Rollison. 'What's wonderful?'

They stared at him, patently puzzled. Neither of them spoke for a moment and then both burst out together:

'Why, the news.'

'I haven't heard it,' said Rollison.

Thereupon they burst forth with good tidings. The eight o'clock news had announced that the onslaught on the Continent promised more than well and behind it there was more than the anticipatory exultation which had been noticeable in some military spokesmen since the beginning of the war. The Americans had earned their share of the general laudations with another smashing blow at Japanese naval and air strength and reduced the Japs to squeals of retaliation and unparalleled ferocity in defence where they were being attacked.

Sitting back in his chair, Rollison nodded slowly.

'That's fine,' he said. 'Even though I've got a headache and a cold in embryo, that's fine.' If they were puzzled by his reception of the news they were too content to comment upon it. He pulled the telephone towards him. Although he did not fully realise it, the secondhand reports had cheered him and were fast colouring his own mood.

Grice was on the other end of the wire a few seconds later.

'This is Rollison again,' said the Toff, very much more himself.

'You got some more sleep, I hope? . . . Oh, too bad! but you'll get over it. Now, I've got a job that will test your ingenuity. Can you get into the building here without being seen? . . . wear disguises, if you want to, but I need to talk in strict confidence and I don't want to come there . . . good man, yes, half an hour will do fine.'

Finished, he went out of the office to that of his CO, an officer of personality and efficiency who had been on the retired list but was fast convincing those who knew him that youth had no copyright of vigour and driving force. A broad-shouldered, red-faced man who looked the typical *pukka sahib*, few belied their appearances more effectively.

'Hallo, Rollison,' said the CO. 'Better news this morning, eh? We need a bit of something like this.' Leaning back in his chair behind a vast glass-topped desk with maps all about the walls of a large, airy room, he frowned a little. 'You're looking under the weather,' he declared. 'Sickening for a cold?'

'Bless this cold,' thought Rollison and contrived a smile.

'Outside influences are worrying me more than a cold,' he said. 'I don't know what you'll think of this but I'd very much like a few days off.'

The CO's mouth positively dropped open.

'Leave? *Now!*'

'Well, if not leave, an arrangement by which I can come in at odd hours,' said Rollison desperately. 'I haven't gone mad or become obstructive, I—'

'Now, look here,' said the CO firmly and uncompromisingly. 'I know that you were at Scotland Yard yesterday, one of my orderlies saw you go in. And I also know that you'd rather be working with the Yard than sitting on your fanny and doing what you do but we can't help that just now, Rollison. In a week or ten days, perhaps, we can arrange something. Sit on your hopes firmly and forget whatever's interesting you now.'

Rollison had a moment's respite when the CO, as if to soften his attitude, pushed across a box of cigarettes.

'Thanks,' said Rollison and lit one. Then his mind cooled, his manner eased, the tension which had possessed him since he had left the flat faded enough for him to smile with genuine amusement as he went on: 'The question is, am I more use alive than dead?'

He made the CO gape again and followed up the advantage quickly:

'For breakfast I had a visit from four incipient murderers and—' he pushed his arm forward and showed the bruises already darkening on his wrist, turned his head and showed another forming on his right temple. 'There are some of the results. I didn't go into this show, it came to me. If you ask me to tell you what it's about I couldn't even begin, except that someone thinks I've got a black box and won't believe me when I tell them I haven't. They won't respect pressure of work at the office; they'll weigh in with all they've got unless I find a means of coping with them.'

He wanted to shake the CO and it appeared that he had succeeded for the other's red face grew redder and his bristling white moustache even quivered.

'Confound you, Rollison, you almost

96

convince me. But—'

Then he broke off.

The expression in his eyes puzzled Rollison, for it merged bewilderment with incredulity. He leaned forward and peered into Rollison's eyes and then exuded a long, slow breath, before pulling a drawer open at his desk and pushing his hand inside.

'Amazing,' he said. 'It really is. This came for you half an hour ago—I was downstairs when a man brought it in and thought I might as well give it you myself. Amazing!' he added and drew his hand from the drawer, clutching a small black box, not unlike a jewel case, with edges sealed with brown gummed paper and a small address label stuck in one corner. 'Is that what you're talking about?'

CHAPTER NINE

GRICE IS OBLIGING

Rollison took the box like a man in a dream, eyeing it and then the CO and breathing so softly that his lungs seemed to be compressed. Holding the box in both hands, but without touching the paper edges or the label, he leaned back in his chair and said oddly:

'Of course it isn't true. I'm dreaming, you're dreaming. This isn't the box.'

97

'Well, it came for you,' said the CO.

'But—' began Rollison, and then swallowed hard. 'This is the most fantastic business I've ever struck, sir. Who the devil sent the thing to me here?' He explained briefly that the quartet of incipient murderers had believed he had the box, that he had known nothing about it but had pretended to hold it and he felt better when the CO nodded as if he fully comprehended.

'Aren't you going to open it?' the CO demanded.

'It's not a bad idea,' said Rollison. 'On the other hand—' He eyed the other blankly and was greeted by a scowl.

'Oh, all right, all right, you don't want me to see what's in it. One way and the other it looks as if you'd better get off and finish with the business before you start work again; if you try to do both things you'll probably fumble 'em both.' The CO was gruff. 'Have a word with Bimbleton and ask him to keep things going as well as he can. What about your girls—they're all right, aren't they?'

'They couldn't be better,' boasted Rollison. 'I can manage all right, sir, provided you'll arrange with Bimbleton to handle anything urgent if I'm not here. I'll give the girls instructions, too. Thanks a lot, sir.'

'You're a damned plausible fellow,' grumbled the CO. 'Good luck, Rolly, and don't get yourself hurt—any more,' he added

98

hastily and smiled as Rollison rubbed his temple and went out.

Rollison clutched the black case tightly as he walked to his office, put it carefully on his desk and rang the bell for the girls. He was brief and just sufficiently apologetic while making it clear that although his temporary absence would be unavoidable, he was quite sure that they would be able to handle whatever transpired without referring too often to Colonel Bimbleton; they assured him in unison that they could and he dictated some letters before there was a tap on the door and Grice entered.

Rollison waved him to a chair and the girl away.

'I haven't a lot of time,' said the Superintendent without preamble. 'I'm assuming you didn't send for me just for a chat.'

Rollison, feeling very much better, beamed at him.

'As a matter of fact, Bill, things have turned up and this and that has happened. You ought to know about most of it but before I go into that will you say "Yes" or "No" if some names I mention mean anything to you?'

Grice nodded, eyeing the Toff suspiciously, saying clearly but without words that he wondered what particular joke the other was about to spring.

'Thanks,' said Rollison. 'Brett, Christian

99

name not known.'

'I know several Bretts,' Grice told him.

'This one is oldish and has recently started on, or is about to start on, a journey with a business mission to America.'

He had not expected to get much reaction from the Superintendent by the mere utterance of names but it seemed to him the best way of making sure that the names meant nothing to the police. Had he expected to create a sensation he could not have been more satisfied for the usually placid policeman started up in his chair then actually jumped to his feet.

'*That* Brett!'

'So I'm told,' said Rollison mildly. 'So it rings a bell.'

'Where the deuce did you get hold of Lancelot Brett's name?' demanded Grice more quietly, resuming his chair and giving the impression that he wished he had not revealed such feeling. '*He* can't be concerned with the Jameson business. What else are you on?'

'Just the Jameson business.'

Grice ran a hand over his thin brown hair as Rollison continued:

'Does Brett mean so much?'

'We-ell,' said Grice quietly, 'he's consulted us several times and to put it bluntly he's been a confounded nuisance.' Grice, a man who rarely used epithets, relied on emphasis for effect and obtained it then. 'He thought at one time that his life was in danger and asked for police protection. We gave it to him. Nothing happened. He pretended that several things did but his statements were at variance with our men's who were watching him all the time. He pitched one ripe yarn about being pushed off a bridge at Maidenhead. He was under survey when he crossed the bridge and all he did was to walk over it and stand looking down at the Thames for five minutes.'

'Well, well,' commented Rollison. 'A persecution complex.'

'It wouldn't have mattered so much in another man,' said Grice. 'We would have referred him to a psychiatrist and left it at that. But Brett is an expert in commercial economics; he has one of the clearest business brains in the country. Being a consultant to the Ministry of Supply, we had to nurse him. He left for the States by air three days ago and I haven't been so relieved to see the back of anyone in my life. Now—' Grice paused to consider and added with feeling: 'You're trying to tell me that he's mixed up in the Jameson business. Come on, what do you know?'

'Wait a minute,' urged Rollison. 'Brett caused a sensation; let's see if we can find a little earthquake as a savoury. Peveril—does Peveril mean anything to you?'

Grice pursed his lips.

'No-o,' he said.

'That isn't convincing,' said Rollison.

101

'I have heard the name,' said Grice, 'but I don't remember in what connection. It's a Cornish name, isn't it? He reflected for a while and then shook his head. 'It doesn't mean anything but I've heard it lately.'

'It could have been in *l'affaire* Brett,' suggested the Toff.

'Or a hundred-and-one other jobs,' said Grice.

'All right, please yourself. Lancing?'

'A town in Sussex,' said Grice.

'Now the police are being clever,' murmured Rollison, 'and they're never so unbearable as then. This time it's a girl named Lancing. I've only met her casually,' he added mendaciously, 'but she could be connected with Peveril.' He paused. 'Nothing clicks? All right, what about Ibbetson?'

'Ibbetson?'

'Yes. Don't you say it well?'

'Don't be an ass,' said Grice, eyeing Rollison warily. 'You know where the name Ibbetson cropped up as well as I do. He was the man whose car Jameson stole last night—I mean the night before last.'

Rollison put his head on one side thoughtfully.

'Is that an established fact? Jameson stole? Or is it a police theory because there's no one else convenient to hang the job on?'

'It isn't proved,' admitted Grice, 'but I've interrogated Jameson and his parents and I'm not particularly satisfied. I've found the pub where he had his drinks and the landlord says that he was drunk most of the time—the kind of drinking when a man sets out to make himself blind.'

'H'm,' said Rollison. 'He'd do anything to forget, is that the idea?'

'Yes.'

'So Jameson's story doesn't stand up,' murmured Rollison. 'That's a pity, I hoped that it would. Did he go back and talk about lost equipment?'

'He did but there was no evidence that he lost it,' said Grice. 'The landlord and two barmaids remember him clearly. He sat in a corner and just drank on steadily, not getting violently drunk but taking enough for the landlord to refuse to serve him after an hour on the second night. What happened there, Rollison, is that young Jameson got an attack of nerves and planned to desert. The actual first steps scared him, so he drank himself into a stupor and the after effects brought temporary insanity. That's not the medical jargon but you know what I mean.'

Rollison regarded him silently for some seconds and then slowly shook his head.

'No, it won't work. There's more in it than that, whether Jameson is our man or not. Ibbetson, whose car was stolen, is risking charges of attempted murder to get hold of a small black case which your Lancelot Brett lost before he went to America.' He avoided telling the full story for the time being, preferring to wait until he had given more attention to the girl's part, and went on: 'Ibbetson thought I had it, the Lord knows why. He came to the flat and a bit later I'll show you the mess he made of it. Was it coincidence that Ibbetson was waiting for the Commando to steal his car or was it a put up job? Was the car waiting there, not to be stolen by a madman but to be used for the getaway after a series of deliberate murders?'

'Ibbetson!' repeated Grice, almost inarticulately.

'I've given you the bald details,' said Rollison. 'And I'll give you more. When I called at the office yesterday it was simply because the affair intrigued me—I saw the improbabilities of the man taking the particular road he did. You probably think I had stumbled on something earlier but I knew just nothing. Despite my virgin innocence someone unknown not only told Ibbetson that I had the black case but sent it to me. Here it is.' He put a finger on the case and looked into Grice's startled eyes, deriving no satisfaction from putting the policeman out of countenance but seeing the complexities of the affair more vividly than he had done before. 'It was sent to me here by special messenger and my CO took it in and handed it to me, sealed as it's sealed now. Would you care to open it?'

Grice picked up the case slowly.

The cover was of Moroccan leather, or a good imitation, and had a poor surface for fingerprints except for the sealed paper and the address label. Grice was careful to hold the case without touching the paper, as Rollison had been.

'Not until I've been over it for prints,' he said. 'Are you serious? Was it addressed to you here?'

'It was and it gave me one of the shocks of my life,' admitted Rollison. 'On the other hand, it made the CO decide that he could spare me at odd intervals.' His smile was positively cherubic and most of the effect of his shaking-up at the flat was gone. 'So hand-in-hand we march, oh Grice, and as always I'm at your service.'

'When are you going to tell me the full story?' demanded Grice sceptically. 'I don't believe I've had anything like all.'

'You haven't,' admitted Rollison frankly. 'But it's going to take too much time just now and there should be another bulletin after twelve o'clock. That is zero hour,' he confided, leaning over the desk and lowering his voice. 'Ibbetson tells me that he's going to have the case from me at twelve *pip emma* or I'm going to die. A forceful man but I don't take everything he says at its face value.'

Grice glanced at his watch quickly.

'Twelve o'clock? If you mean that—'

'Now, hold it,' protested the Toff. 'Every half-word I utter this morning you view with scepticism and I've done nothing but tell you the truth. That was his threat. He was so sure I had the case that I admitted it and told him it was at the office. I fixed an appointment outside the flat for twelve sharp.'

'I'll get it watched at once,' said Grice, obviously struggling to retain his equanimity and to accept what the Toff told him as gospel truth. 'How many men do you think you'll need?'

'None,' said Rollison firmly.

'Don't be a fool.' Grice was nearly irritable.

'None,' repeated the Toff more firmly. 'If I judged Ibbetson aright, he'll know a Yard man by sight and smell and I don't propose to take chances with him. I'm going to hand him a case. What's the time? . . . nearly eleven; then we've three-quarters of an hour to get a black case as like that one as two peas, labelled and gummed up in exactly the same way for me to hand over to Ibbetson or his courier. Can do?'

'Even if I can, the man needs following,' said Grice.

'Oh, no. I know at least one place where he lives. We don't want him followed; we want him to think that he scared me effectively, at least until he's opened the case.' Rollison leaned forward and touched Grice's hand. There was a note of appeal in his voice and there was no doubt at all that he was in dead earnest. 'Don't abide by regulations and upset this chance. You know as well as I do that if we do the wrong thing just now we might really get into a mess. If you'd like a metaphor, the case is like a bud just opening and if we pull the stem we'll never get the full bloom.'

Grice scowled at him.

'That's a beautiful picture but—' He paused, shrugged his shoulders and eyed the case, not Rollison. Rollison's wrist-watch ticked audibly but, apart from that, there was no sound in the office.

Rollison wondered whether he had tried Grice too far; he knew that, of the men at the Yard, Grice was the only one on whom he could rely to be unorthodox; in consequence, the Toff was more frank with the Superintendent than with any of the others. Until then he had been given no reason to repent his frankness but as he watched the man deliberating he wondered whether Grice would come down heavily with his official foot and insist on watching Rollison and the flat.

Grice looked up at last, his eyes very wide.

'All right, I'll see you this far.'

'Good man,' said Rollison gratefully. 'You had me scared; I was already deciding never again to confide in a policeman! What about a replica of that case? Do you think you can manage it?'

'It's got to be done,' said Grice. He stood up, and added: 'Have you an envelope large enough for this?' Rollison found one and Grice inserted the case carefully, sealed the envelope and then nodded. 'I'll have the new one sent round here, shall I?'

'Please,' said Rollison. 'And thanks again.'

He felt annoyed that he had not thought of handing a dummy case to Ibbetson or Ibbetson's envoy before; the time was short and supplies of leather goods were at a low ebb. He even doubted whether Grice would contrive to get approximately what was wanted and although he dictated several letters he kept his eye on the clock. If he travelled by taxi he would want at least fifteen minutes after leaving his desk to reach the flat at noon and at twenty minutes to twelve no one had arrived.

Three minutes later his telephone rang and Grice spoke briskly.

'It's waiting for you in the commissionaire's box, Rolly.'

'Saved by a hair's breadth,' said Rollison, with satisfaction, 'or rescued by the police. Thrilling adventures of an amateur detective, episode nine.' He dropped facetiousness and added: 'Bill, you'll play fair?'

'I'm leaving it to you this time,' Grice assured him.

'I'll be seeing you,' said Rollison and pushed his chair back, saying to the girl sitting by him: 'I'll have to finish that later. If I'm not in this afternoon I'll telephone a message. Cheerio!

And remember the poet's advice to sweet maids.'

'Goodbye,' said the girl faintly.

The commissionaire had the case, wrapped neatly in brown paper, and handed it to Rollison as the latter passed with a smile and a word of thanks. Several taxis were in sight outside the building and he jumped on the running board of the nearest as it slowed down. He was on the crest of a wave of excitement and confidence, enough in itself to warn him to go carefully, but he sat back in the cab and took the brown paper from the dummy case, wondering even then if Grice had contrived to get a duplicate good enough to deceive anyone who knew it by sight. When he saw the brown gummed paper sealing the edges and the white, addressed label, he silently congratulated Grice and then reflected that he needed some plan of campaign.

Ibbetson's messenger was not likely to take the case, say 'Thanks' and then hurry off. There was at least a chance that the case would have to be opened in his presence and Rollison was pondering how to evade the difficulties that such a possibility engendered when the taxi drew up outside his flat.

He climbed out, paid the driver and looked about him.

Two or three people were in sight but they approached and passed, showing no interest in him or in the case; the paper wrapping remained in the cab. His exhilaration fading, Rollison glanced at his watch and also heard a clock striking twelve; he was there to the moment and no one could complain about that.

Then he saw Ibbetson.

He was astonished that the man dared to come in person but there was no possibility of a mistake. The plump man wore the same suit of light grey and hurried along with short steps, eyeing the Toff and the case in his hand. Some degree of bargaining was called for, of course, and Rollison kept a firm hold on the case, tucking it under his arm as the other pulled up in front of him.

'Got it?' demanded Ibbetson abruptly.

'Haven't you eyes?' demanded the Toff and took the case from beneath his arm. Ibbetson's hand moved to take it but he kept it firmly and said: 'It's not going to be quite as easy as that. This is a bargain and there are two sides to it. What are you offering?'

'Now, listen to me,' said Ibbetson and his queer light eyes were round and hard. 'Mike's at the other end of the street and if there's any funny business he'll use a gun. I didn't take this chance without being prepared, Mr Ruddy Rollison. I know you think you're smart but you can't outsmart me. You haven't got any dicks in sight, none has come into the street in the past two hours. I made sure o' that. So hand if over.'

Involuntarily, Rollison glanced over his shoulder.

Ibbetson was not lying; at the far end of the street, thirty yards away and within easy shooting distance, 'Mike' was standing idly with his right hand in his pocket. On the opposite corner stood Charley, probably fondling his knife. Ibbetson was confident that he could handle the situation capably, relied on his aides and was sure that the show of force would silence any argument Rollison wanted to make. The calm effrontery of the man was disturbing but, as far as Rollison was concerned, this was what was wanted. Ibbetson could have the case and then the chase would start in earnest.

'Look here—' he began, putting up a show of argument for the sake of it.

'Gimme,' said Ibbetson. 'I've allowed you three minutes—they're nearly up.'

As he spoke a car turned into the other end of Gresham Street. It was a small two-seater with the hood down and, although Rollison saw it, it did not register on his mind. Ibbetson's expression was clearly calculated to intimidate him and there was no purpose in refusing to be intimidated. He held the case forward and Ibbetson's fingers gripped it. Both of them held it for a moment, Rollison pretending reluctance to let it go. Ibbetson strengthened his hold, tugged it away and then half-turned.

111

As he did so the car pulled up alongside them.

A large, heavily-built and florid-faced man was at the wheel, with dark hair and dark, jutting eyebrows. Rollison caught a glimpse of him and heard a little squeal of brakes. Then the driver leaned over the side of the car, stretching out a long arm and a hairy hand. He took the case from Ibbetson quickly and without a fuss, tossed it over his shoulder into the back of the car and trod on the accelerator. The small car roared forward; the whole thing happened so swiftly that Rollison had little time for thinking; but as he saw the car move past and heard the oath on Ibbetson's lips, Rollison flung himself to the ground, anticipating shooting.

'Mike' used the gun at once, firing from his pocket but his first shots were directed towards the car, not the Toff.

CHAPTER TEN

SOME HOPE OF SALVAGE

Ibbetson was swearing deep in his throat when he began to run in the wake of the car. Rollison rolled closer to the house which was denuded of iron railings but with a small ridge of stone work where they had been embedded before the war time drive for scrap iron. He was thinking only of the man who had so neatly lifted the case and the possibility of being used as a target but, as he heard a bullet strike the wing of the small car without stopping it, he rose to his feet and backed into the porch of the house.

He took out his service revolver while, on the other side of the road, a woman with a perambulator began to run, tight-lipped, in the opposite direction.

From an open window a man said clearly:

'What the devil!'

Rollison saw Ibbetson tearing along on his short, stubby legs, Mike firing towards the car and the driver nearing the corner as if impervious to danger or at least ignoring it; the back of his head seemed a black mat of hair. He slowed down a little as he reached the corner and swung round on two wheels. He went so near the opposite corner that Mike leapt away and his next shot was spoiled. The engine snorted, the exhaust gave out a cloud of dark blue smoke and the thief disappeared from sight.

No one appeared interested in Rollison.

Grice would condemn him for not shooting to wound Ibbetson or the other gunman but he saw no point in that then; he preferred to let the men escape unless they were caught by policemen on beat duty or by passers-by. His immediate fear was that, in their anxiety to get

113

away, Ibbetson and Mike might start another orgy of shooting like that in Chiswick.

Rollison left the cover of the porch and hurried after Ibbetson who had reached the corner and swung round it, his coat-tails flying behind him. From the end of the street there came the snort of another engine and a taxi passed. Mike was on the running-board, opening the door. Ibbetson jumped in and fell into the back. Dexterously Mike following him inside and then the taxi gained speed and went on, presumably in the wake of the two-seater.

At the corner, Rollison was in time to see the taxi disappearing into Piccadilly; there was no sign of the smaller car.

Rollison re-holstered his revolver, turned and strolled back towards the flat. The terrace was crowded with people who had rushed from the houses and passers-by who had gathered as if by magic from nearby streets.

A neighbour who knew Rollison, and much of what he did, snapped at him harshly:

'I wish to heaven you'd move, you're always making trouble!'

'Not I,' returned Rollison placidly. 'Others make the trouble, I try to stop it.'

'Pah!' exclaimed the neighbour, a tall, long-moustached man who affected high-winged collars and long cigars. 'What happened?'

'Someone shot at someone,' said Rollison vaguely. 'Dangerous things, firearms, they ought to be banned.' He raised a hand in

114

amiable salutation and walked to the house, going up the stairs slowly and thoughtfully.

No one was on the landing.

There were scratches on the lock of the front door but probably they had been made when the thieves had first forced entry and there was nothing to be judged from them. He opened the door quietly, pushed it open and stood aside. There was no sound, no hint of movement. Revolver in hand again, he entered the foyer and stood listening. The silence was complete, no rustle of movement reached him. He frowned at the sight of the ruined furniture and general chaos but ignored that long enough to look into every room, examining it closely: the flat was empty, Ibbetson had set no further trap.

'Or,' decided Rollison, 'no obvious one. That man is getting me worried; he'll start using infernal machines before he's finished.'

Nevertheless he felt reasonably secure, although very rueful after his further survey of the damage. No bed was fit to sleep on, hardly a chair offered any comfort. He was reluctant to move to a hotel for the night but was contemplating the possibility as he moved to the telephone. He called Harridges and was soon talking to a quiet-voiced man in the Furniture Salon. He put the position fairly: if he, the man at Harridges, was called upon to furnish a five-roomed flat at short notice with reasonably good furniture, could he do it?

115

'It is possible, sir,' said 'Harridges' softly, 'but it would be expensive. Our range of goods—'

'Just for once, never mind expense,' said Rollison recklessly.

The gentle voice grew warmer and enthusiastic. The goods were there, ready for inspection at any time. Rollison corrected him promptly: he did not want an inspection of the furniture but delivery that afternoon, plus the services of several men and an empty van to remove some damaged goods before the new furniture was delivered. The soft voice thought that perhaps he had best come to see the flat to better estimate the requirements. Delivery that afternoon was asking rather a lot but in a case of real necessity.

'If you must come, come at once,' implored Rollison.

The soft voice declared that it would and took the address.

Rollison had not closed the door of the flat while telephoning and had been aware of footsteps approaching and a shadow on the threshold. There was nothing menacing about the approach or the shadow and, when he replaced the receiver and turned, he saw Grice standing with his hands in his pockets regarding the disorder. On the Superintendent's ascetic face there was an expression not so much of stupefaction as of incredulity, as if Grice were looking at

116

something which could not be.

'Hallo,' said Rollison cheerfully. 'Gaze upon the result of the visit from four human tornadoes. It was quite a breeze, wasn't it? All this for the little black case which proves that they needed it badly.'

'I've never—' began Grice, seeking a suitable adjective, and then threw his hands towards the ceiling. 'I've never seen its equal in my life! Was this all done this morning?'

'Some of it under my own eyes,' admitted Rollison mournfully. 'There were some cherished pieces, too, but nothing that really mattered is beyond repair. A furniture man is coming to put me to rights shortly and you'll be able to convince him of my *bona fides*. Have a drink?'

'No thanks,' said Grice, still looking dazed.

'And you can't even find the spirit to ask me what happened at zero hour,' said Rollison, in a rare good humour. 'I'll volunteer a statement that'll give you time to gape and gloat. I came here with the dummy case. Ibbetson met me outside and after a short argument I handed it over. Then on to the scene pounced another human cyclone, complete with an MG two-seater. He grabbed the case and careered off and, after some fireworks, Ibbetson and the others followed him in a cab which probably doesn't ply for hire in the approved fashion. We do see life, don't we?'

Grice pulled himself together.

'I had a word with a constable outside and gathered what had happened. Did Ibbetson say anything else?'

'Except to threaten me with extermination if I didn't hand over, no,' said Rollison. 'He had his preparations well in hand but he was nervy and wanted to get the case and be off. Whether he had a surprise packet waiting for me I don't know but the intruder took the limelight and I just watched and waited—after taking due precautions, of course.'

'Couldn't you have stopped them?' demanded Grice. 'Or even one of them?'

'Probably,' admitted Rollison. 'Ibbetson runs like a duck; he was very nearly a sitting bird.'

'Then why the devil—'

'Grice, Grice!' remonstrated Rollison. 'When I first knew you anything approaching strong language was verboten, you were nothing like a policeman at all. Now you're almost running true to type. Of course I didn't stop them or try to. We don't want them stopped yet; we want to find out what it's all about and you won't do that by cross-examining Ibbetson or his brood. Let's be reasonable about this show, if nothing else. Are you sure you won't have that drink? I know you're the most abstemious man at the Yard but in the circumstances—'

'I'll have a lime juice, if you've got one,' said Grice, smoothing his hair. His taut skin, with its odd, transparent look, was slightly flushed and his movements towards what was left of an easy chair were quick and mechanical. 'I'm trying to believe all this, you know.'

Rollison mixed a lime juice and soda then poured a lager for himself. The fire was burning well and the windows were closed against the cold. They sat on hardwood chairs and Rollison eyed the other whimsically.

'You aren't trying to believe this, you're trying to convince yourself that I know a lot more than I've admitted. I don't. I've heard funny stories but that's not evidence and I've introduced you to the new Ibbetson, the real Ibbetson. You'll try to trace him, of course; you have to do that but I think he'll be well enough under cover to dodge you for a while.'

'Don't sound so pleased about it,' grunted Grice.

'I *am* pleased about it,' said Rollison blandly. 'If you arrest Ibbetson now we may never get right to the bottom of it and you know that as well as I do. But as an officer of Scotland Yard, with presumptive evidence of Ibbetson's waywardness, you have to look for him. I suppose,' he added hopefully.

Grice regarded him without favour.

'Why are you so anxious that we shouldn't get any of them?'

'I'm not. I just want the day for the darbies delayed,' Rollison assured him. 'You remember my beautiful allegory about the bud

119

and the flower? The midday sun has brought a swelling of the bud but the bloom isn't out yet. Still, you're the policeman. Of course, the only evidence you have against Ibbetson is what I've told you and hearsay doesn't really amount to evidence.'

'I've a clear-sighted policeman who saw him running after the car,' said Grice heavily.

'But not shooting or otherwise misbehaving. As far as the policeman is concerned Ibbetson, whom he wouldn't know by name anyhow, was the victim. Hang it, no one can blame a man for chasing after another who had snatched a valuable Moroccan case from his hands. But that's up to you,' continued Rollison. 'I've made it pretty evident now that I think Ibbetson would be better on a long leash than in Cannon Row. As for why—well, who employs Ibbetson? That has its place in the scheme of things.'

'Ibbetson would probably talk if there is an employer, which is purely guesswork on your part,' opined Grice. 'Isn't it?' he added sharply.

'Not guesswork, no. Deduction, or whatever word you like to use. The Ibbetsons of the world don't work for themselves; they organise, they plan, they execute but they don't get the major part of the rake-off or they wouldn't go about London as the OC of a pernicious little mob. Besides, there are other indications, you know. All Ibbetson wanted

120

was the case. He was satisfied at the sight of it and showed no desire to look inside. That might have been because he thought things were hotting up for him but it's as likely that he didn't want to look inside because the contents didn't interest him. Ibbetson's job was to get the black case and, but for the dark-haired man who manoeuvred the car so neatly, he would have had it. Talking of getting cases, have you looked inside the original yet?'

'No,' said Grice. 'I haven't had time.'

'You only just kept to the letter of the agreement,' Rollison reproached him. 'You were here by twelve-thirty but at least it was too late to do any damage. You'll let me know what's in it, won't you?'

'Ye-es,' said Grice. 'Are you sure it's Brett's?'

'I'm told it is.'

'Who told you?'

'Let's say the daughter of a Rumanian prince,' beamed Rollison with bland humour. 'But don't look as impatient with me as that, old man; I'm as much at sixes and sevens as you are and I always did talk a farrago of nonsense when things wouldn't work out as smoothly as I'd like them to.'

'Only then?' demanded Grice sarcastically.

He showed a disposition to stay and was there when a small dapper man in morning clothes tapped on the front door, to be admitted flourishing a card from Harridges.

Rollison watched his round, bland face as he surveyed the lounge. Few men could have seen such a sight; lining, webbing, and springs were spread about in confusion, there was a litter of papers, feathers from a cushion which had been slit open, a disorder of disorders shown in sharp contrast against the well-dressed Grice and Rollison in uniform. But the owner of the soft voice did not widen his eyes while he surveyed the scene but slowly inclined his head.

'I think I see what you require, sir. If I may make a suggestion, it would not be economic to replace all of the pieces here. Many of them can be repaired and I can assure you that they will be as serviceable and attractive as before they were damaged. In view of the shortage of furniture, may I suggest that you have just what you need for the time being and allow us to take the damaged articles to our workshops?'

'Do that,' said Rollison.

'Thank you, sir. Would you care to advise me which pieces you feel in need of immediate replacement?'

'Two beds and some easy chairs and other obvious necessaries will be all right,' he said. 'I haven't time to go into detail.'

'Will someone be here all the afternoon to receive our men?'

Rollison widened his eyes and Grice smiled ironically.

'I'll lend you a man, Rolly.'

'Thank you,' said Rollison, knowing that Grice would like nothing better than to station one of his men at the flat for the rest of the day. There was no workable alternative, however, and Grice left to arrange for the man while Rollison prepared a snack in the kitchen and made further half-hearted attempts to tidy it up.

He was fully aware that Grice was dissatisfied and unconvinced of his ignorance of the affair until the previous day and, with each incident, the justification for Grice's suspicions grew. To Rollison that mattered little; so far as he could judge the next real step would be made after he knew the contents of the Moroccan case and there was little that he could do until Grice telephoned him. He preferred not to visit the bomb-damaged block of flats where June Lancing lived and where Ibbetson had a flat—although it was possible that Ibbetson had moved already. Not greatly concerned by the likely difficulties of tracing Ibbetson, Rollison spent an hour considering all that had happened, finally deciding that three things were of paramount importance; the others were incidental.

The three items were:

(a) Why had Brett given the case to June Lancing?
(b) What was in the case and had Brett

expected it to be a source of trouble?

(c)   Who was the man who had stolen the dummy?

'I might add "why do the other folk want it?"' commented Rollison *sotto voce*, 'and then answers to that questionnaire will cover most of the matters arising. I wonder how long Grice's man will be?'

He had expected the man from the Yard to arrive earlier but, as it happened, he was there alone when a man in a green baize apron knocked at the front door. Before that, Rollison had seen outside a large van with *Harridges* painted in tall letters on its side and consequently he had no doubts of the man's identity.

The caller was the foreman of a party of four oldish, grey-haired men who had none of the soft-voiced salesman's sublime tact but commented forcefully on what they saw. Then they stared at Rollison and the foreman exclaimed:

'Did someone *lose* something, sir?'

'I did hear talk about a needle,' replied Rollison amiably. 'Do what you can to tidy it up for me, will you?'

'*Tidy* it! Why, yes, sir.' The foreman eyed a pound note that Rollison took from his pocket and added warmly: 'We'll do everything we can to 'elp, sir, but we've got to be out by four, the new stuff will be 'ere by then.'

'That'll do fine,' Rollison assured him.

Watching them at work, he felt an increasing desire to go to Gower Street and see June Lancing.

Earlier in the day he had convinced himself that he would devote every spare minute to the office; but the attraction diminished and he assured himself that the two girls and Bimbleton would manage very well. He was putting on his coat when he heard footsteps on the stairs, loud because all the doors were open for the easier removal of the damaged furniture.

The footsteps were heavy but not laboured. The newcomer was in a tearing hurry, shouting before he reached the landing and condemning two men and a large easy chair to perdition. Rollison strolled towards the reception lounge in time to see a big man force himself past the removers and reach the top stair. He wore a heavy, belted tweed coat, tight about his thick figure; his dark eyes were aflame with anger, his dark hair was dishevelled and his clear, jutting eyebrows thrust themselves forward.

'What the devil's happening here?' he roared. 'Who's moving? This is Rollison's flat, isn't it? Why the blazes can't you take that thing out of my way?' he shouted at the foreman who was carrying a small fireside chair with its springs gaping. 'Here, who did that?'

'Ask me,' said the foreman and went onwards.

Rollison stood expressionlessly on the threshold, eyeing the storming newcomer whom he had seen once before and whom he judged to be Peveril—the man who had snatched the black case from Ibbetson's grasp. Peveril saw him and his brows knitted closer together. He thrust his right hand inside his coat and drew out the dummy case with pieces of the gummed sealing paper adhering to the sides.

'Are you Rollison?' he demanded aggressively.

Rollison was incisive and cold.

'I am. Is this your usual method of approach?'

'Oh, don't bandy words with me,' roared the newcomer. 'What the devil do you mean by this? It's not the real case, it's a fake. I'll have you know that you can't get away with it.' He pitched the case on to a nearby chair and stood squarely in front of the Toff, bellicose and bristling.

Rollison eyed him up and down and then jabbed him in the stomach, a gentle blow but enough to make him gasp and back away.

CHAPTER ELEVEN

SHOWDOWN WITH PEVERIL

The temptation to take any course which would deflate the man had been too strong for Rollison to resist. He prepared himself for a wild blow in return and was not disappointed. The other uttered a grunt of sheer astonishment then swept his right hand forward in a clumsy swing which missed by inches. Rollison went in close and jabbed more sharply in exactly the same place as before. The other bent forward, presenting a massive chin invitingly. Rollison resisted the further temptation and gripped the man's right wrist.

'Do we have to brawl?' he demanded coldly.

'B-brawl! I'd dam' well like to know who started it!'

'If you must argue, keep your voice down,' said Rollison. 'Do you want all these people to hear?' He indicated the returning Harridges men and led the visitor firmly through the flat to the kitchen. Once inside, he closed the door and leaned against the refrigerator. His companion stared about the small, white-tiled room, swallowed hard and gasped.

'Where—where do you think you're taking me?'

'To the only room in the flat not upside-down,' said Rollison. He proffered cigarettes, knowing that he had the blustering newcomer at a disadvantage and confident that he could retain it. He recalled June Lancing's comment on the description she had 'heard' of Peveril and there was ample justification for thinking that it applied to this man. What amazed Rollison was that he should have the brazen nerve to come after the incident of little more than two hours before when he must have been seen by several neighbours.

Startled, the other took a cigarette.

'Now what's this nonsense about the wrong case?' demanded Rollison, flicking twice at his lighter before getting a flame. 'And before we go any further, you're Peveril, aren't you?'

The heavy face showed amazement; the cigarette, half-way to his lips, was held in fingers which went rigid. Hoarsely, and after a pause, he demanded:

'How in the name of Confucius do you know that?'

'We needn't drag in third parties,' said Rollison, straight-faced. 'You're Peveril and you've a lot of explaining to do. A description of you has been circulated throughout England after the shooting outside here this morning. This is the one place in the world that you should have avoided just now.'

'I didn't shoot anyone,' snapped Peveril. 'I—but lookee here, I'm not going to be browbeaten by you; that case was a dummy

128

and I want to know the meaning of it.' His effort to regain the initiative was accompanied by a ferocious scowl but he glanced covertly at Rollison's right hand.

The Toff concealed a smile.

'More to the point is how you knew that it would be exchanged downstairs,' he said sharply.

'I overheard that fool Ibbetson telling his men,' answered Peveril. 'The man hasn't the sense to keep his mouth shut.'

The Toff narrowed his eyes and said sardonically:

'I suppose you've got a flat next to his and because the walls have been damaged by bombs you can overhear everything they say?'

Just as Grice had been completely taken aback by the name 'Brett,' so Peveril was stupefied by the supposition. Before he made any comment Rollison knew that it was so, that the girl's story of a flat next to Ibbetson's was to be repeated by Peveril. He changed his approach swiftly, making it seem that he knew that Peveril had such a flat and interrupting a flow of 'how do you knows' from the big man whose composure, sadly disturbed by the greeting, was completely disintegrated by what seemed a demonstration of uncanny omniscience.

Without his bombast, Peveril was a more normal and even likeable individual; at first sight Rollison had judged him to be nearer

129

fifty than forty but his manner was that of a pretentious and yet naïve schoolboy; a youngster of twenty would have talked with greater maturity.

Rapidly it dawned upon Rollison that Peveril's manner, the competition for the case, even the nature of the attacks and the ruthlessness of the Ibbetson company, were alike less intriguing than a single fact which emerged from Peveril's five-minute discourse, a rambling one which, however, always came back to the point without reminders from Rollison. The single fact might have been of negligible importance to anyone else, although certainly it would have interested Grice.

Peveril assumed that Rollison knew all that there was to know about the case.

To a lesser degree, Ibbetson had worked on the same assumption but then Rollison had assumed that Peveril had given that impression to the plump man. The idea could hardly be self-conceived and nurtured; someone else had undoubtedly planted the seed in Peveril's mind.

Rollison's difficulty grew more formidable. Would he be wiser to admit his ignorance by asking Peveril for information or would it be better to let the other man continue to think that he knew everything, gleaning crumbs of information until he was able to build the whole loaf? He might have decided on the former but for the fact that his supposed knowledge was the main factor in Peveril's subjugation.

Peveril said hoarsely:

'D'you know, Rollison, I've heard about you but damn if I ever believed half of it. How do you get to know these things? You weren't even on the job forty-eight hours ago.'

'This is progress,' thought Rollison and eyed the other without smiling. His expression was almost contemptuous as he waved his hand, saying aloud: 'It's my habit to know all there is to know about a case before I start it.'

Peveril's slate grey eyes were genuinely confused.

'But how could you, this time?' he mumbled. 'I didn't think anyone knew it except Brett, Lancaster and me. Damn it, the whole thing was an absolute secret; it couldn't have leaked out!'

'Ibbetson seems to have learned a little,' said Rollison drily and a moment later knew that he had come close to tumbling his own house of cards.

'Don't be an ass,' said Peveril sharply. 'Ibbetson is with Lancaster. When those two had a swearing match and Brett did a double-cross, Lancaster nearly went mad. By Mahomet, I've never seen a man go purple before! Brett's a bit of a fool, really; he ought to know that he's no match for Lancaster but you know what these big business men are. They don't believe anyone living can teach

131

them anything.'

Peveril paused, eyeing Rollison steadily, giving a hint that just then he was not so ingenuous as he had been a few minutes before. Rollison shifted his position and made a shot in the dark.

'Brett was playing pretty safe. He knew that he was going overseas.'

'Eh?' ejaculated Peveril. 'Overseas?' His eyes narrowed, and he backed a pace, knocking against the wall. Rollison saw his eyebrows knit together and his own heart began to hammer. Obviously he had made a serious blunder but he could not imagine how. Peveril swallowed hard and then recovered. 'Er—oh, yes, of course. D'you know, I didn't think of that.' He uttered a low-pitched and insincere laugh and stubbed out his cigarette in a waste-dish in the sink. 'By Confucius, that's a fact! Poor old Lancaster! Try one of these,' he added and took out his cigarette-case, holding it towards Rollison and at the same time pushing one cigarette closer to the other man.

Rollison took the cigarette, disturbed by the change in the other's manner but not failing to see the manoeuvre with the case. It might be the gesture of a man making it more convenient for another to take a cigarette but it could mean that Peveril was deliberately ensuring that Rollison took a particular one.

'Thanks,' said Rollison. He extracted and

then dropped it. 'Oh, damn!' He moved his foot but clumsily trod on the little white cylinder then looked quickly into Peveril's eyes: the man's expression conveyed nothing as he said:

'Don't worry, plenty here.'

'It's my turn,' declared Rollison, taking one of his own cigarettes but accepting a light before plunging on with a statement of fact which might serve to confuse the other. 'There are things I don't know and—'

'What, even you?' demanded Peveril sardonically. He laughed again, on the same note of insincerity. 'I don't believe it! Anyhow, a joke's a joke and perhaps you were right to give Ibbetson the wrong case, but where's the real one?'

'Do I look as simple as that?' demanded Rollison.

'Simple?' echoed Peveril, frowning. 'You know darned well that I've as much right as anybody to the case. What's worrying you? It can't make any difference to Brett or Lancaster if I get it. I've taken some chances on this business and I don't mean to lose out. It's worth a cool five thousand to me and five thousand pounds is a lot of money. Hand it over and don't be bloody-minded.'

Rollison drew on his cigarette slowly and then shook his head.

'No,' he said. 'Too much hangs on it for it to be as simple as that.'

133

'It's no business of yours!'

'If you're going to get bellicose again you may as well go home,' said Rollison. 'I'm not handing the case over to you until I know a lot more about it.' He was burning to ask how Peveril knew that he had had the case and why the man was so sure that he would be ready to hand it over. 'In fact, I'm not letting anyone else have it until the affair is over and Ibbetson and his brood are put where they can do no more harm. That isn't a specious hope but a statement of firm intent,' he added. 'The point at issue is whether you're going to continue playing a solo hand or whether you're coming in with me.'

Peveril kept quite still.

He was a striking figure, thought Rollison dispassionately, with his dark eyebrows jutting so fiercely and very red lips pushed slightly forward; with a pointed beard he would belong to Drake and Raleigh's generation; he needed only the correct habiliment to look the image of a lusty buccaneer; about him there was a tang of the sea, his manner that of a man who rejected compromise, discipline and the ordinary things. It was a fleeting thought and passed while Peveril tightened his lips and clenched his hands; his cigarette jutted from one corner of his mouth aggressively.

'So *that's* your game,' he said softly. 'You want a cut in this.'

'It depends what you mean by a cut,'

retorted Rollison promptly. 'The stakes are high.'

'That five thousand is coming to *me*,' snapped Peveril, 'and no-one else.' A little pulse in his neck was beating fast and he looked likely to develop a fit of tearing rage, so the Toff tensed himself to repel attack. Instead, Peveril went on more reasonably, although his voice was harsh. 'All right, all right, if that's your game I'll see you but I know my way about. I'm a practising solicitor and don't forget it. All you've done is to hold the case for a few hours. I'll give you a hundred, *after* I've collected the prize money.'

Gently the Toff shook his head.

'No can do,' he said. 'Not even for a peculiar lawyer like you. Just glance about the flat and ask how far a hundred will go in putting that right. And I've been assaulted,' he added with well-feigned indignation, 'both beaten about the head and bent about the elbows. A hundred be damned, this isn't a bridge party.'

'Two hundred,' said Peveril between his teeth. 'Not a penny more. Come on, take it or leave it.'

'No,' said Rollison quietly. 'There's no deal until the Ibbetson family are where they belong and the other things are cleared up, Peveril. You forget that money isn't everything, even in this material world. I will hold the box.'

'You damned well won't!'

The Toff waved a hand about the kitchen and said:

'All right, go and get it.'

'Now listen to me, you barefaced twister, I'll break every bone in your perishing body if you don't come across.' Peveril leaned forward, large enough to tower above the Toff who remained leaning negligently against the refrigerator and maintained an aggravating smile. The other's voice rose and grew in volume. 'I know just how to deal with your marrow-muscled type, blast you, and I'm not leaving here without the case! Two hundred and fifty, that's my absolute limit, and if you don't accept I'll—'

Rollison slipped past him and opened the kitchen door. He was not surprised to see the foreman and one of the men standing in the outer room and staring indeterminately at the door; neither moved as the Toff appeared but the foreman said hesitantly:

'You needing any 'elp, sir?'

'I might do soon,' admitted Rollison amiably, 'but I think you'll be sufficient as a moral support. Peveril, we aren't having a boxing match, we're being reasonable. I've told you when the box or case will be available and that will be only if you're good. If you've a line of patter other than threats I'll listen. If you haven't, clear out. I've a lot to do.'

'You can't do this to *me*,' breathed Peveril.

'I am doing it to you,' returned the Toff blandly. 'And even with pleasure.' He watched the changing emotions on the man's face, imagined that Peveril was trying to find a way of climbing down without it developing into a rout.

Shrugging, Peveril passed him.

The Toff followed him to the landing as two of the removal men arrived at the head of the stairs; the flat was practically empty of damaged goods and was looking tidy, if denuded. Peveril's heavy breathing made the most sound until Rollison caught his elbow as he started for the stairs.

'Just one thing,' he said. 'How did you know I had the case, Peveril? Telepathy, or secret information?'

'Bah!' ejaculated Peveril, 'you make me sick!'

He hurried down the stairs as forcefully as he had climbed them. The Toff watched him disappearing and then called over his shoulder to the foreman: 'Stay here until I come back, will you, or until a man comes with a pass from Scotland Yard?'

'*Strewth*!' he heard. 'Er—okay, sir, we'll 'ang around.'

The front door banged before Rollison started to speak and there was little likelihood that Peveril had overheard the request. Rollison hurried to the ground floor and into the terrace, seeing Peveril striding towards the far end of the street, his great shoulders swinging and long legs covering the pavement with enormous strides. Rollison waited until the man turned the corner, seeing him glance back once, and then hurried in his wake. He wanted badly to know where Peveril would go and needed a talk with the man in circumstances different from those at the flat where too many people could listen in.

Reaching the corner, he saw a Scotland Yard sergeant in plain clothes who pulled up as the Toff appeared.

'I can't stop,' said Rollison as he passed, assuming this was Grice's man. 'Carry on to the flat.' He did not wait for a yea or a nay but reached Piccadilly in time to see Peveril going through the gates into Green Park.

Peveril walked like a man who knew exactly where he was going and who had a definite purpose in mind. His progress was so bull-headed that the Toff wondered whether it meant all that it appeared to on the surface. They crossed the park and soon were in Victoria Street, Peveril allowed to keep about thirty yards ahead all the time. At Vauxhall Bridge Road Peveril turned left, leaving the clock and the station on his right and walking several hundred yards before going left again into a street of tall, narrow houses, many of which had white cards announcing *'Apartments'* or *'Bed and Breakfast.'* Peveril entered the fifth house along and Rollison saw him disappear.

Rollison would have followed but for the man he saw at the other end of the street; it was Ibbetson.

Backing into the main road swiftly but peering round the wall of the corner house, the Toff watched Ibbetson raise his chubby hand in a gesture which brought the thick-set Fred from the porch of another house. Together they hurried to that which Peveril had entered, neither of them looking back nor giving the impression that they suspected that Peveril might have company.

'I might hear something to my advantage here,' mused the Toff and hummed the air from the *Warsaw Concerto* as he gave both men ample time to disappear into the house and then walked the length of the street, noting that the thoroughfare was called Queen's Place and the house was Number 9.

No porch-way hid Charley or Mike, whom he considered with respect, and there were no loungers in a street which ran along the bottom of the thoroughfare. Satisfied that he was not likely to be taken by surprise, yet wondering whether his precautions were sufficient, he returned and entered in the wake of Peveril, Ibbetson, and Fred.

The first thing that surprised him was the silence.

In an apartment house at such a time there were usually sounds from the kitchen or else the murmur of voices. He heard nothing, not even the stealthiest of footsteps. He peered along a narrow passage to the closed door of what he presumed to be the kitchen and then glanced at the stairs; they were narrow but looked solid and boasted a thick carpet. Walking up them with little sound, he passed the empty first landing and then carefully approached the second; that, too, was empty. Moving with even greater stealth he approached the third, and last, landing. Half-way up the top flight of stairs he saw Ibbetson's legs, clad in light grey, and those of another man, both standing against a door. The faintest of scratching sound followed and then Ibbetson moved forward; the door opened very slowly and the silence was like an enshrouding blanket.

Then a clear voice, filled with fury which was under control, said viciously:

'I thought you'd fall for it. Come in and put your hands up!'

There was a gasp from Ibbetson and Fred turned and ran for the stairs. They had planned a surprise but been taken off their guard. Fred did not notice Rollison until he was nearly on him and then all the Toff needed to do was to put out a leg: Fred stumbled over it and crashed down the stairs while Peveril continued in the same sibilant voice:

'Never mind him, it's *you* I want.'

Ibbetson went into the room and the door closed, while the Toff vacillated between going up farther and listening in and hurrying down to Fred, who was lying on the floor with his eyes closed.

CHAPTER TWELVE

HALF CIRCLE

The toff had rarely wished more urgently for Jolly who could have taken Fred away and kept him in a safe place while the conference proceeded upstairs. The door of Peveril's apartment had hardly closed, however, before he was moving downstairs. At all costs he must prevent his flank from being left open to attack; when Fred recovered the man was not likely to be idle.

Looking about him from the landing, the Toff saw a door standing ajar; in the poor light he read the white word BATH on a brown door. 'That might be useful,' he said *sotto voce*.

Stepping over the man's unconscious figure he glanced into a bathroom so dingy that it looked as if the residents rarely used it. Little more than a square box-room with just room for the bath and small hand-basin, it was gloomy because the window was covered with blackout paper turned green in patches and torn in others. The bath itself was a tall, old-fashioned tub with water-marks of generations on its sides. Wrinkling his nose with distaste, Rollison went out after taking the key from the inside of the door and half-carried, half-dragged Ibbetson's man into the bathroom. He took off the victim's tie, bound his wrists behind him and then lifted him into the bath; it was not comfortable but there was little chance of the man escaping without outside help. Rollison gagged him with a handkerchief, tested the knot of the tie and went out and locked the door.

Going upstairs he put the key in his hip-pocket and took out his own keycase, selecting the skeleton key as he approached Peveril's door. There he could hear a murmur of voices but he did not think they came from the room immediately beyond the door. He picked the lock, taking less than thirty seconds, a far more successful effort than when he had opened his own lounge.

The front room, a lounge of fair proportions, was empty; voices sounding much stronger but still not clear came from a door on the right. Rollison glanced about him and pulled a chair towards the door, jamming it under the handle and thus making sure that no one could enter furtively or surreptitiously.

By the second door he heard Peveril's voice.

'Shut your foul mouth! I'm doing the talking.' Peveril paused as if to give Ibbetson an opportunity for defying him then went on: 'If you worked for me, you congenital bungler, you'd be out on your neck in double-quick time. I thought you had the case but you let Rollison put one across you. It was a dummy. Understand that, you half-wit, it was a dummy! A fine story you'd have had to tell, *if* you'd got that far. Now you'll have to go and whine to Lancaster and admit that I beat you to it. You won't tell him that you were fooled but I'll find a way of letting him know.'

Ibbetson put in unsteadily:

'I don't know what you're talking about. Who—who's Lancaster? I don't know—'

A sound that seemed like a slap followed. Rollison imagined Ibbetson receiving the treatment he had so freely meted out and a pleased smile curved his lips.

'I'm not dumb,' snapped Peveril. 'You work for Lancaster. The poor fool thinks that I'll back out but I'll beat him to it. My market for the case is bigger than yours. I don't work for chicken-feed. Go back to him and tell him that if he doesn't get out of the market and take you with him there'll be more trouble brewing than he'll want to take, the yellow-bellied numbskull.' Peveril drew a deep breath, apparently to recover after the invective and then went on harshly: 'As for you, if you come near me again I'll split your skull. And listen, keep clear of Rollison. I'll handle him. There isn't room for the two of us and the one who

143

stands down isn't going to be me, even if I don't need a gang of cut-throats to do my work for me. Have you got all that?'

Ibbetson started to say something but was cut short by a bellow from Peveril. The Toff heard a heavy thud and then heavier footsteps. A sound of a scuffle followed and the door shook. The Toff looked about him swiftly and saw another door, standing ajar. He retreated to it and went inside a small bedroom, disappearing as the first door opened after moving away the chair.

Peveril towered above Ibbetson, whom he held by the scruff of the neck with a casual ease which would have been funny in different circumstances. Ibbetson's mouth was gaping like a fish, he looked as if he were choking. Peveril forced him across the room, held him while he opened the front door and then rushed him to the head of the stairs. The noise as the two men raced down shook the old house, fading only a little as they descended the first flight of stairs. A shout followed and then a greater rumbling noise; the Toff imagined that Ibbetson was being thrown down the bottom flight of steps.

Peveril bellowed abuse which must have reached the ears of passers-by; but the words were lost on the Toff who waited for a few moments then left his hiding-place and went into the room where Peveril and Ibbetson had been talking. It was a study with several easy chairs and a cocktail cabinet standing open and revealing an array of bottles rare in war time.

Footsteps on the stairs warned him that Peveril would soon return.

Dispassionately the Toff had admired Peveril's treatment of the plump crook but about their interview there had been something which rang false. He could not place it; nor could he reconcile Peveril's mouthing and talk of violence with his comparatively mild treatment of Ibbetson: after such a threat something more than a run out of the flat would have been fitting.

Thinking of that, the Toff backed behind the door. He heard Peveril striding across the outer room and the door bounced back on him; he caught the handle to prevent it swinging to and making his presence obvious. Peveril stepped to a modern steel desk in front of a window and stood peering into the street for what seemed a long time. He had both hands thrust in his pockets and his attitude was not that of an elated man.

When he swung round his brows were knit and his scowl ferocious. That was until he saw the Toff; then his lips dropped open and he gaped.

'G-good gad!' he exclaimed.

'That's mild for you, isn't it?' asked the Toff amiably. 'I thought you'd pull something out of the bag for a special occasion.' He took his revolver from its holster slowly and deliberately and held it pointing towards the thick, dark brown carpet. All the time he watched the other's face and, just as the recent interview had struck him as false, so did Peveril's expression. The man's slate-grey eyes held a cunning glint; he registered surprise so convincingly that it was overdone.

'M-mild!' gasped Peveril.

'That's what I said,' said the Toff. 'Do you know June Lancing? No? A pity, she's a nice girl. I was telling her one day that when people don't act true to form they become suspect. You aren't running true to form. I wonder why?'

'What—what did you expect?' Peveril said thickly.

'Oh, a fine old rodomontade of invective,' said the Toff, 'with an occasional reference to Confucius and Mohamet.' He smiled widely, reaching a chair and leaning against it as he went on softly: 'Do you know, Peveril, I'm beginning to rate you higher than I did at first. You expected me, didn't you?'

'Expected!' ejaculated Peveril.

'Expected,' repeated the Toff. 'You thought I would follow you and accordingly you treated Ibbetson mildly. Had you done him real violence with a third party in the neighbourhood it might have been risky. Not bad, Peveril, you do quite well.'

'You're talking a lot of nonsense!' snapped

Peveril. 'Put that gun away, you don't need it.'

'You mean that you hope I won't need to use it,' corrected the Toff. 'We'll see. It depends on how you behave. Who are you working for?'

'None of your business,' said Peveril harshly.

'I'm making it mine.'

'You won't find out anything from me.'

'Oh, I don't know,' said Rollison, 'you've told me a lot already. More perhaps than you realise but we'll go further into that later. The question that really matters at the moment is: "How did you know I had the black case?"'

Peveril scowled but looked less aggressive, even surprised and a little sceptical.

'You aren't serious about that.'

'I'm so serious that if you don't tell me I shall get violent with you,' Rollison assured him. 'It's a simple question: how did you know?'

'By Jupiter, you're serious! Why, Patrushka told me.'

'Who?' exclaimed Rollison, startled.

'Patrushka.'

'Oh,' said Rollison blankly. 'Of course, that explains everything but if I knew anyone named Patrushka it would be a help. As I don't, you'll have to try again. This time,' he added with a firmer note in his voice, 'don't use a mental pin to stick in a name to pass on to me.'

'But she did tell me!' insisted Peveril. 'I had

147

to wring it out of her, she was as stubborn as a mule but I put a scare into her and she told me she'd sent it to you. I didn't know that the little swine Ibbetson was listening in,' continued Peveril darkly. 'If I had, I'd have been at the flat a lot earlier than he was but you handled him all right.'

Rollison made no immediate comment but admitted the possibility that Peveril believed that what he was saying to be true. He raised an eyebrow above the other and then mused:

'I shall have to get to know Patrushka but, before that, tell me a little more of what she told you.'

'This is just damned silly!' exploded Peveril and then went on quickly at the sight of a gleam in Rollison's eye and the slight raising of the revolver. 'Oh, all right. She told me that you were interested in the case and were looking after the case for her until she reclaimed it or sent a messenger for it. I thought it was going to be easy but Ibbetson stole my thunder. You would have had an uncomfortable morning if I'd arrived first. Ibbetson doesn't know the first thing about persuasion.'

'Remembering his efforts on me, I'm glad you were late,' said the Toff ironically. 'So I was looking after the case for the unknown Patrushka. She—' He stopped abruptly, drew a deep breath and then snapped: 'What does she look like? Has she got cloudy blue eyes, dark hair worn in a page-boy bob, short upper lip and nose? And does she dress well and—' he paused and found inspiration, 'wear a three-diamond ring on her engagement finger?'

'Now what the devil are you trying to do?' demanded Peveril. 'If this is your idea of getting me confused, it won't work. Of course that's Patrushka. Who do you think it is?'

The Toff did not confide that he thought the girl was June Lancing.

CHAPTER THIRTEEN

THE TRIBULATIONS OF JOLLY

If the Toff's expression relaxed enough for Peveril to see that his equanimity was momentarily shaken, Peveril made no comment. The Toff rubbed the fingers of his left hand along the barrel of his revolver, making the other back a pace and knock against the window.

'Are you really as frightened as all that of a gun?' murmured the Toff. 'It isn't like you; too many people aren't acting as they should. Including Patrushka.' Much of what had happened was beginning to make sense and he contemplated the wisdom of forcing the interview with Peveril a stage further when there was a sudden, high-pitched scream from beneath the flat.

It came so abruptly and with so little warning that even Rollison turned his head. But Peveril was too startled to turn the carelessness to his advantage.

'What's that?' he demanded hoarsely. 'What was it?'

'We needn't worry,' said the Toff but altered his mind when there came a loud pattering on the stairs and a woman's voice raised hysterically.

'Murder, murder! Help! Police! Murder, murder!'

'What the devil's happened?' snapped Peveril. 'We can't stay here doing nothing!'

'I shouldn't let it worry you,' said the Toff. 'Someone has chosen this afternoon, of all times, to have a bath.' He cut short Peveril's abrupt interruption, adding sharply: 'I used the bathroom for Ibbetson's bosom friend, Fred. I also locked the door.'

'All the tenants have keys,' muttered Peveril, turning pale. 'Was—was he all right?'

'He wasn't dead when I left him, if that's what you mean,' said Rollison. 'Nor was he conscious or comfortable. I wish that woman would stop screaming,' he added testily.

The woman's cries remained shrill and high-pitched although they sounded farther away. Heavier footsteps followed on the stairs and a door banged open. Then a man's voice came after a moment of silence so acute that it made

150

Rollison and Peveril stare at each other, animosity forgotten in uncertainty.

'My God!' exclaimed the speaker. 'Get away, Lucy, you don't want to see this. Send—send for the police.'

With one accord Rollison and Peveril stepped through the lounge to the landing. Hurrying down the stairs to the bathroom, they saw the door wide open. A woman in a dressing-gown of bright hues was hurrying down the next flight of stairs while a man's shoulders blocked the door. Rollison reached him and asked mildly:

'Can I help?'

'Eh?' A heavily-built man with two or three days' growth of stubble on his face, dressed in the uniform of the AFS, turned sharply. His eyes reflected shock and horror and his lips twitched. 'Er—no, I don't think so. Look at that.'

Over his shoulder both Rollison and Peveril peered towards the bath: only the torso and legs of Ibbetson's "Fred" were visible at first but on the top of the dirty sides of the bath were bright red stains. Tight-lipped, Rollison craned his neck so that he could see the man's head and shoulders.

Someone had cut Fred's throat.

Whoever had committed the crime had made no nicely judged cut but had slashed with vigour. Rollison saw the man's head lolling backwards, remembered how he had

151

bundled him into the bath and left him helpless. While he had been talking to Peveril the murderer had stalked; and Rollison could conceive only one reason for the murder: Fred as a prisoner, perhaps under arrest, might have talked: that risk had been liquidated.

'You said—' began Peveril hoarsely.

Rollison dug an elbow sharply into his stomach, making him stop. The AFS man was staring fascinatedly at the gruesome sight and did not notice the byplay.

'The Yard should know about this at once,' said Rollison. 'Peveril, will you try to make sure that no one leaves the house? I'll send a policeman along as soon as I see one.'

He turned without waiting for an answer and hurried down towards the street. The crisp, cold air was welcome and refreshing. From the downstairs flat he heard a woman speaking urgently, presumably into the telephone, and in the room opposite another woman was sobbing hysterically.

The Toff hurried past and turned towards the Vauxhall Bridge Road. He had gone a hundred yards or more before seeing and beckoning a policeman in uniform who stopped and saluted.

'Did you want me, sir?'

'You're wanted at Number 9, Queen's Place,' said Rollison quietly. 'It's not nice, constable, in fact, it's murder. If you're wise you'll keep an eye on the occupant of the top flat. I'm going to see Superintendent Grice immediately.'

Without waiting for a response, but silently congratulating the constable on the calm way in which he reacted, the Toff hurried to the nearest telephone kiosk and from it dialled the Yard. He was disappointed, for Grice was out. He made a brief report to another Superintendent—who promised immediate action—and added:

'I've asked a local constable to keep an eye on a man named Peveril who lives at the top of the house. I was going to ask Grice to get a search warrant for his rooms before this happened. This will be a good opportunity but don't start to build a case against him. He didn't do it.'

'Are you sure, Mr Rollison?'

'He was with me when the man was killed,' Rollison assured him and rang off.

He had no regard for Fred and, until the moment of peering over the AFS man's shoulder, had contemplated the prospect of doing violence to the thick-set man with some eagerness. The sight of the blood-red gash, and the knowledge of Fred's complete helplessness when he had been killed, gave him an uncomfortable feeling of self-reproach. It was useless to make assumptions but it seemed that Ibbetson was responsible for the murder and he no longer cared whether Grice put out a call for the plump man or not. He had tried hard to find just what was behind the affair before any definite steps were taken but there were limits to the patience of the police and to the risks he dare take.

He took a taxi to Gresham Terrace, pondering on the conversation between Peveril and Ibbetson and his conviction that Peveril had almost certainly expected to be followed. He did not try to solve the problems presented by that tortuous-minded solicitor but considered the man Lancaster, who now loomed as large in the affair as Lancelot Brett.

It was nearly five o'clock when he reached the Terrace.

A smaller Harridge's van was standing outside and when he approached his flat he heard voices, the deep one of Grice's sergeant alternating with the suave tones of the quiet-voiced man who had acted so expeditiously and proved that Harridges did indeed provide exemplary service. Entering, Rollison nodded to the salesman who approached with his hands fluttering gently and saying obsequiously:

'I felt that I should come to make sure that everything was to your satisfaction, sir.'

'Ah, yes,' said Rollison. 'A very good job, thanks.'

For the first time the little man was slightly out of countenance, as he said gratefully:

'I'm glad that you think so, sir. Perhaps I may have the privilege of showing you—'

154

'Thanks, no,' said Rollison, and smiled distantly. 'I'm sorry. My preoccupations don't include furniture at the moment but everything looks fine.' The lounge, in fact, was resplendent with new easy chairs and two settees which looked the acme of comfort; the hour and a half since he had left had seen a miracle performed. 'I'll let you know if there's anything else,' he added. 'Goodbye.'

'Goodbye, sir,' echoed the soft voice faintly and the man went towards the door. Standing by it, he cast one surprised and reproachful look over his shoulder, then squared them and went firmly outside.

The heavy features of Grice's sergeant were turned with stolid curiosity towards the Toff.

'You do get things done, sir, don't you?'

'Get things done?' ejaculated the Toff bitterly. 'I vacillate, I hesitate, I start a dozen things and finish none of them. Get things done be damned, I—' He pulled himself up with a start and shrugged his shoulders. 'All right, all right, it's simply a matter of opinion. I'm going to have a drink,' he added firmly. 'Care to join me?'

'Thank you, sir, but it's rather early for me.'

'It's far too early for me,' declared Rollison but went into the dining-alcove, mixed himself a whisky and soda and drank it deeply. Then he lit a cigarette and the action reminded him of the cigarette he had dropped from Peveril's case. He went through the flat tempestuously,

155

leaving the sergeant staring at him perplexedly and found that the kitchen had been scrupulously tidied. He muttered an imprecation and called: 'Sergeant, at the double!'

The sergeant obliged but remained bewildered.

'Who cleared this up? There was a cigarette squashed on the floor and I want it.'

'A cigarette?' echoed the sergeant.

'Yes. I trod on it. And I'm not the arch-priest of anti-waste; it must be analysed.' Opening the kitchen door, Rollison stepped to the iron landing of the back stairs and pulled off the lid of the dustbin. 'Any luck, sir?' asked the sergeant anxiously.

'I do believe there is,' acknowledged Rollison, his tension easing as he stooped down and retrieved the trodden cigarette which was on the top of a pile of dust and rubble. 'The gods relent sometimes, even for me. I won't need you here now,' he added, after a pause. 'Take this with fear and trembling to the Yard and get it analysed as soon as you can, will you? It may be just Virginian tobacco mixed with choicest Eastern blends, as we're always assured on the packets but, whether or no, have copies of the analysis sent to Superintendent Grice and to me.' He paused and then relaxed with a smile. 'That's if you don't mind.'

'Of course not, sir.' The sergeant put the

cigarette into a small envelope he took from his pocket, looked lingeringly about the flat, picked up his hat and went out after asking whether Mr Rollison was sure that there was nothing more he could do.

Rollison spent a few minutes contemplating each room. Harridges had left nothing undone and he made a mental note to pay the soft-voiced salesman a visit of congratulation.

'But not until this is over,' he added *sotto voce* and stepped to the telephone, picking up the directory and glancing through the LANs. There were too many Lancasters for him to hope to select the right one and he did not propose to ring each number on the chance of having some luck.

'If only I knew why Peveril was so sure that I would hand the black case over,' said Rollison aloud. 'And why he kept switching his reactions. And why June-Patrushka lied to me.' He considered the possibility that Peveril had done all the lying, shrugged the thought away and then heard footsteps outside. They were brisk and yet sedate, the familiar approach of Jolly.

Rollison stepped towards the door, listening for an indication that the girl was with him but, when he opened the door, only Jolly was there with a key extended in his hand.

'Thank you, sir,' said Jolly. 'Good evening.'

'Where is she?' demanded Rollison sharply.

'I very much regret, sir, that I cannot tell

157

you,' said Jolly. 'Allow me.' He waited with a hand on the door for Rollison to go back into the flat, followed, removed his hat, muffler and coat with a deliberation which set Rollison's nerves on edge and then eyed his employer frankly. There was little expression on his dyspeptic face but he lifted his hands in a gesture of resignation rare in him. 'I'm sorry, sir, but at the last moment she evaded me. I am afraid that it was in some measure my responsibility.'

'Oh,' commented Rollison blankly. 'I'd been relying on a talk with the lady.' His disappointment was greater than he allowed Jolly to see: 'When was this?'

'No more than half an hour ago, sir. As we left the office.'

'She mixed with the crowd?'

'Er—yes and no, sir. She did go into the crowd and get separated from me but an oldish gentleman was waiting in a small car for her and she joined him. They went off together and the young lady turned and waved to me.' The very flatness of Jolly's tone expressed the degree of his mortification and was enough to make Rollison smile faintly. It was easy to imagine Jolly's feelings when she had turned and waved, almost certainly mockingly, after he had faithfully kept her company all day.

'An oldish man and a small car,' Rollison mused.

'A distinguished-looking gentleman,' elaborated Jolly, 'and the number of the car was FX 21K. I assure you that Miss Lancing appeared so appreciative of your kindness during the day that I felt quite sure that she would return willingly with me. It was not so much a case of me keeping near her, sir, as of her keeping close to me. She was good enough to initiate me into the particular work which we were executing and she expressed her pleasure at my proficiency.' Jolly took a deep breath. 'I was completely deceived, I'm afraid.'

'We both were. What was the work like?'

'It was simply the sorting of mail,' Jolly assured him, 'and she was right in one respect at least, the office is considerably understaffed. The Commandant went so far as to ask me whether I could spare an hour or two each day to go along and help during busy spells, such as this, but I was, of course, evasive in my answer. And after Miss Lancing's duplicity my interest in the work is hardly what it was. There is a possibility that she will return there tomorrow, of course,' he added, without much hope.

'It could be. Was she known as June Lancing at the office?'

'Oh, yes, sir.'

'Not as Patrushka?'

'Patrushka?' echoed Jolly, puzzled.

'I won't go into that again,' said Rollison hastily. 'Obviously she wasn't.'

159

He explained what Peveril had told him of 'Patrushka' and went into considerable detail about the affairs of the day. It was always restful to make reports to Jolly who was a listener in a thousand but who occasionally made comments which were both shrewd and pertinent. Jolly heard him out, interjecting only a congratulatory comment when he mentioned that he had been able to get released from the office and, as he talked, Rollison considered the problems presented in a fresh light, feeling much less jaded than he had.

He finished and then went to mix himself another drink.

Jolly was sitting back in an easy chair when he returned, regarding him thoughtfully. When Rollison invited Jolly to sit down it was not his man's habit to perch on the edge of the chair and look ill at ease and he did not alter his habit then. His expression was grave and his eyes thoughtful as he said:

'What conclusions have you reached, sir?'

'None,' said Rollison promptly. 'What are yours?'

'I haven't really had time to assimilate everything thoroughly,' said Jolly slowly, 'but I am a thousand times more regretful that I allowed the young lady to get away. We need so much to find out how she knew that the case had been sent to you.'

'We need that more than anything else,'

160

admitted Rollison. 'Confound it, she didn't guess! And no one sent the black case to me just for the sake of me or because they remembered someone who had heard of me. And—'. He paused, his head on one side. 'Jolly, the Ibbetson connection keeps this affair in line with young Tom Jameson. Apart from Ibbetson, there's no connection; that's the *prima facie* evidence, isn't it?'

'Undoubtedly,' admitted Jolly.

'But there's more,' snapped Rollison, jumping to his feet and striding across the room. 'There's much more, Jolly, but I've only just seen it. Only the Jamesons, father, mother and son, knew that I was involved in the case even remotely, except the police. Remember that black case was posted last night to the Delivery Agency and all I'd done then was to see Grice and have a chat with him and go to the canal cottage. This morning the whole world knew that I was interested and that the case had been sent to me. Conclusion: the Jamesons gave the information away. No one else could possibly have known on what case I was working—and I wasn't even working on it then.'

'I'm not sure that your assumptions are fully justified, sir,' said Jolly carefully. 'You may have been seen entering the cottage.'

'Seen and recognised?' demanded Rollison. 'I don't think it's likely. And there's another thing. Young Jameson told me a story that I

161

was inclined to believe but the evidence wouldn't support it when Grice made inquiries. The story fell down on the lack of corroboration from the landlord and barmaids of a pub near the canal. That lack of corroboration could have been deliberate. Grice did give me the name of the pub,' he added and broke off, snapping his fingers, and staring at Jolly for inspiration. 'Confound it, the name was connected with the canal, it— I've got it! The Bargee. Have you had anything to eat?'

'I'm not particularly hungry,' said Jolly.

'You can probably get a snack at The Bargee. Hurry down there and get a feel of the place. The men you might see are—' He gave brief, but sufficient, word pictures of Ibbetson's two companions—since he had interviewed Ibbetson he did not need a description of the plump man—and added: 'Go carefully and remember that if Ibbetson sees you he'll probably connect you with me and that won't be healthy. Perhaps I'd better send a policeman with you, in case of accidents.'

'I hope you will *not*, sir,' said Jolly emphatically.

'All right, please yourself and get back as soon as you can.'

'Will you be staying here, sir?'

'Of course not. I'm going to see the Jamesons,' declared the Toff. 'I'll beat you to

162

it but we're going different ways. Grice will probably be here soon, so we'd better hurry or he'll delay us too long.'

On the crest of a wave of excitement, which he afterwards admitted to be unjustified, Rollison left the flat five minutes after Jolly. A taxi was depositing a fare outside a house nearby and he hailed it immediately. Once inside he saw a closed car turn the corner and glimpsed Grice sitting in the tonneau; two men were in front. Grice's expression was grim and Rollison raised an eyebrow as he considered the likely import of questions which the Superintendent would have ready for him. The journey to Wembley took a little more than forty minutes, fair going by road and at least equal in time to the same journey by train.

'Stay here, will you?' Rollison asked the driver.

The man had pulled up outside a narrow cut which led from the road running alongside the canal to the canal itself. It was dark and only the sidelights of the cab showed, together with the bright gleams of the stars high in a cloudless sky. Although it remained cold, Rollison did not think that it was so piercing as it had been on the two previous evenings; but he walked carefully along the canal bank towards the cottage which, once he was past the advertising hoarding, showed in clear silhouette against the stars. There was no glimmer of light from the cottage and, although he knew that the blackout restrictions made that normal, he could not repress a fear that his quarry was out.

He shone his torch, finding a knocker but no bell. The knocker was a light one of brass and made only a slight sound, hardly enough to arouse anyone inside. There was no response and he tried again. A second period of waiting made him exclaim in annoyance and then he banged heavily on the door with his clenched fist.

At last he heard a movement inside.

His annoyance faded and he even prepared a smile with which to greet one or the other of the elder Jamesons when a door slammed and he heard a rough oath, followed by footsteps outside the house near the back. He went to the path swiftly and heard a clatter of footsteps, followed by whispered voices. He could not be sure but he thought that one was Ibbetson's. Unable to see the men, he went closer to the corner of the house and heard their breathing as they approached.

By day he had seen that the only entrance to the garden was from the little gate close to the canal but he was prepared for them to rush over the garden and jump the fence, rather than be orthodox and resort to the path.

Then a torch shone out in front of him.

Its powerful bream broke all the lighting restrictions and bathed him and the side of the house in a bright glow. He blinked against it, backed closer to the house with narrowed eyes, prepared to deal with an assault but knowing that he had been caught at a severe disadvantage.

To counteract it, he shone his own torch.

He caught a glimpse of Ibbetson and two other men, one of them carrying a body over his shoulder; the light was good enough for the Toff to see a pair of shapely legs dangling in front of the man before one of the others fired at him.

CHAPTER FOURTEEN

IMMERSION BY NIGHT

The shot missed him and struck a window, the glass breaking and splintering with a loud report. Rollison jumped farther into the garden to get out of the beam of light, reaching for his revolver as he did so. Another shot—obviously the man had a gun fitted with a silencer—came uncomfortably close but by then he had his fingers about his gun and he fired towards the torch. In spite of the odds against him, his aim was better for he struck either his target or the holder's hand and the torch clattered to the ground and went out. By then he had switched off his own torch and the darkness was intense. He heard a man blundering past him and Ibbetson—it *was* Ibbetson—snapped in a high-pitched voice:

'Dump her—dump her in the canal!'

The darkness, breathed Rollison, if only there were light in the darkness. He was treading on soft soil and movement was difficult. He heard blundering footsteps and then an oath, presumably as a man struck against the garden fence. Another bullet, heralded by a flash of flame which only revealed the gunman momentarily, hit the earth yards from the Toff who drew a deep breath and switched on his torch again, knowing that it would give the sharpshooter a much easier target.

The man with the girl was climbing over the fence: Ibbetson was behind him and the third man was standing by the fence with a gun in his hand. His shot and the Toff's were simultaneous and both missed. The Toff moved to one side, leaving the torch on the ground. It shone slightly upwards because it rested on a pile of earth and cast a pale glow about the fence; but it no longer meant danger to him. Making a sweeping movement, he approached the fence while keeping out of the radius of the light.

He reached it as the man carrying the girl threw her into the canal. That eerie scene, with the figures shown as dark silhouettes in the faint light of his torch, was vivid and macabre. He saw every movement of the man

166

who lowered the girl so that, for a moment, he cradled her in his arms then tossed her forward. The light was just sufficient for Rollison to see a flurry of arms and legs but he did not catch a sight of the surging water, although he heard the splash which half-drowned another shot from the gunman by the fence.

'Come on!' howled Ibbetson. 'Hurry!'

The plump man took to his heels, the others followed him and in a moment they were lost in the darkness. Rollison fired in the direction of the running footsteps three times, less in the hope of wounding them than of making sure that the neighbourhood was thoroughly aroused and would rapidly investigate. Then he vaulted the fence and shone his torch on to the water of the canal.

At first he saw nothing.

His heart was beating fast enough to threaten suffocation: he did not think that there was much doubt about the identity of the girl whether she were, in fact, June Lancing or Patrushka. The fact that she appeared to have gone beneath the surface was a frightening thought and he moved the torch so that the light bathed the surface of the water for several yards. Then he saw her face, sideways towards him, and could even pick out her mop of hair which was floating on the water.

'Hold on!' he shouted. 'Hold on!'

It was a wasted exhortation for she was

167

unconscious, floating sluggishly and going farther under with every passing moment. Rollison put the torch carefully on the cement edging of the bank, fearful lest it should roll into the water. Every moment was agonising but he had to have some light. He put his hat by the torch, to prevent it from rolling, and stripped off his greatcoat and tunic while kicking off his shoes.

The girl had floated out of the radius of the torch before he was ready.

He heard confused sounds not far away but did not think of them, did not even assume that they were made by people from the row of houses in the road where the taxi was waiting. He moved the torch gently, holding the hat in position all the time, then picked out the girl's face again. It was half-submerged; he thought that her mouth was under water. But he was satisfied that he could reach her and took a racing dive.

The shock of the immersion in the icy water stung him so much that his head reeled and he felt himself going stiff; he was surprised by the sharpness of it. He did not fight against it but continued to follow through, coming well up within the radius of the light. The girl was floating two yards away from him but he could only see her hair.

Two strokes took him to her.

By then he was shivering; the cold bit to his bones after the few seconds of his immersion but he clenched his chattering teeth, kept his eyes open and stretched out a hand to clutch her hair. It slipped from his fingers but he tried again and pulled her to the surface. As she came up he caught one glimpse of the pallor of her face and then their movement took them outside the light and there was only darkness.

His shivering increased.

He kept afloat with one hand while manoeuvring with the girl with the other. Movement in the water was difficult but she was soon floating on her back: he could feel her face, turned towards the stars, with his free hand. He turned over slowly and cautiously, frightened all the time lest he should lose control of her, but contrived to keep her face upwards and to get himself into a position where he could support her while swimming, also on his back, towards the bank. He remembered the little iron rings built into the concrete for barges and boats to tie up and wondered vaguely whether he would be able to reach one. The cold was growing worse, almost paralysing his legs and arms. Movement was difficult and painful and there were moments when he seemed not to be moving at all but merely trying to, as if he were in the grip of a nightmare hold which would not relax. Mechanically he fought against it, his teeth chattering like castanets. The girl stayed in front of him, her head close to his chin, making no movements of her own volition.

Only then did he try to shout for help.

It was difficult to make his lips form the word and when he uttered a cry the sound was so faint that he knew it could not travel far, even along the surface of the water. Taking a deep breath he tried again; this time the volume was better but he had no idea whether it travelled far enough.

He was fighting a losing physical and mental battle against the cold, so much worse because he had been immersed so suddenly, but the fears of cold and of having to struggle on without assistance faded suddenly into one much greater.

Something clutched at his leg.

He kicked out but his movement was slight and he did not release himself. For a moment he thought that it was a hand and imagined that another would be pressed over his head, forcing him down. Then the truth came to him; weeds were entwined about his legs, holding him.

The darkness about him was impenetrable and the glow of his torch seemed a long way off.

He shouted again, no longer struggling against the weeds with his fast leg but using his arms and his free leg to try to get nearer the bank; reaching and holding one of the iron rings grew all-important. His breathing was short and laboured, even his lungs seemed frozen. He knew that he was growing weaker and that the paralysis of cold which had threatened was becoming a growing menace; he even doubted whether he could reach safety.

Then a light shone on the water near him.

For a second he was so startled that he did nothing but watch it. Then his body twitched and he opened his mouth to shout again. Vaguely, as if from a long way off, voices responded. He thought he heard someone say: '*There he is!*' but could not be sure. He kept still and the light moved until it shone into his eyes, blinding him.

'Hold it!' a man exhorted urgently.

'Where's that hook?' another called.

'Comin', George,' said a third man breathlessly.

To Rollison they seemed a long time, although he knew that they would be in time to reach him. Of greater urgency was the increasing weight of the girl. He put his hand to her chin and found that the water was lapping up to her mouth. He eased her further above the surface and then was seized by a cramp in his right arm and leg. He gasped in pain and did not see the boat-hook which moved gropingly towards him. Another torch was switched on and the hook caught in his shoulder. Tight-lipped, and with increasing spasms of pain coming from the cramp, he could do nothing to help himself but the men on the bank were on their knees with outstretched hands, risking a ducking to bring him and the girl to safety.

They took her first.

One man lay full length on the bank and, leaning close to the water, put a rope about the girl's arms and then slowly hauled her until other hands could reach and lift her to safety. The boat-hook kept Rollison close to the side; without it he believed he would have gone under. He felt an easing of the pain as he was lifted but did not feel the hands gripping him; when at last he was stretched out on the bank he was numbed from head to foot except for the shooting fires of the cramp.

'We've got to get them into 'ot barves, an' *quick*!' a man declared. My missus 'as got the water 'ot, one of 'em can go there. What about yours, George?'

'Soon get it 'ot,' declared the ubiquitous George. 'We could do wiv' them stretchers, wot's Bert thinking of?'

'We ain't 'ad a raid fer so long they've got rusty up at the post,' declared the first speaker with a ghost of a chuckle. 'Wot they reely wants is a nip o' somefink. Wot about 'opping over to The Bargee and getting' a quartern, George?'

'Not me,' said George. 'Mean! They wouldn't squeeze yer a teaspoonful o' gin if you was dying. I never did like that pub an' I never will.'

They were working as they talked, giving the girl artificial respiration and massaging Rollison's stomach and arms. He felt a little warmer while thoughts filtered more coherently through his mind. If he could only get really warm he would be much better; they must not be long taking them to the hot baths. But he was a fool, he had a whisky flask in his hip pocket. He swallowed hard, and then croaked:

'Pocket—flask.'

'What's that, guv'nor?' asked one of the men promptly. 'Eh . . .oh, that's the ticket!' He found the flask and in the light of a torch unscrewed the stopper. A spot of whisky was put to the girl's lips first and then a trickle into Rollison's mouth, biting him but bringing a fiery warmth as it began to course through his veins. In a few minutes he felt much better and by then also they had stopped working on the girl, one man declaring with profound satisfaction that she was breathing like a good 'un. Relief helped to improve Rollison's own condition while stretchers from a nearby first-aid post were soon at hand. Men lifted him gently on to one, although he thought that he was in a good enough condition to walk, and he was carried along the narrow path to the row of little houses.

By then other men had arrived, amongst them a sergeant of the police.

In the front room of a house a large fire was

173

burning and there, for once in his life, Rollison really enjoyed a fug, as he said urgently: 'Sergeant, my name's Rollison. I'm helping Mr Grice—'

'Mr Rollison!' exclaimed the sergeant sharply. 'Oh, *yes*, sir. Can you tell me—'

'Three men, including Ibbetson,' interrupted Rollison, drawing a deep breath. 'Remember that name—Ibbetson. They threw the girl into the water. Now—can you send someone—to the cottage? Canal Cottage. There might be more trouble there.' He paused at an expression of surprise on the man's face and added more sharply: 'What's the matter?'

'The Superintendent's left a man there,' said the sergeant slowly. 'I wonder if—but I'll check up, sir. Anything else?'

'Yes,' urged Rollison. 'Send a man to The Bargee. Ask for a man named Jolly—don't mention my name, just ask for Jolly. If he's there, bring him here at once unless he has any other suggestions to make. Can you—do all that?'

'I'll get started right away, sir.'

It was mortifying to be so useless but the cold was still in the Toff and only a twenty minutes' soaking in a steaming hot bath brought comfort. After the first ten minutes he felt that he had nearly thawed out and even summoned the energy to call to a man waiting outside the bathroom door for a cigarette. He finished it while laying there then towelled

174

himself vigorously and began to wonder why he had felt so weak and helpless for, by then, he was glowing with warmth and felt fit enough to tackle any eventuality. If he were anxious about Jolly and the news from The Bargee he concealed it and thought more of the girl in the next house, hoping that she was being as well cared for as he. He was not yet sure that it was 'Patrushka' but he did not dwell long upon doubts. Dressed in borrowed clothes that were a little too small and tight for him, and wrapping a blanket about him for extra warmth, he left the cottage and went next door. His own clothes were drying in front of a fire tended by the friendly little wife of George.

In the hall of the next house he found a tall, thin, melancholy-looking man with grey beard who eyed him without interest and continued to speak to an angular woman who had opened the door.

'Keep her wrapped up and warm for the night, Mrs Mee, and she will probably be all right tomorrow. Give her that sedative in half an hour and let her sleep as late as she wants to.' He looked away from the angular Mrs Mee and eyed Rollison. 'Do you want me?'

'No thanks, doctor,' said Rollison. 'But I want a word with the young lady upstairs.'

'Is it necessary?' asked the doctor.

'I would say vital,' Rollison assured him.

'Oh, all right, but don't worry her too much.'

The doctor, who looked harassed and tired and was almost certainly overworked, let in a blast of cold air as he left the house.

Mrs Mee regarded the Toff, still wearing the blanket about the borrowed clothes, and asked with a touch of sarcasm whether he was going to stop the night too. Rollison judged quickly that, although she had been quick to offer hospitality and help to the girl, she was worried lest she were called upon to do more. He assured her that he would make sure that she was amply compensated for her trouble. Talk of compensation brought about a change in her manner; she was just going to take a cup of coffee up to the poor young lady, would the gentleman like one, too?

'No, thanks,' said Rollison. 'I've had one next door. Which is the room?'

'I'll show you,' said Mrs Mee.

She led the way up the narrow stairs and into a room leading to the right of a small landing; the lights in the room and the passages were shaded. The girl was lying against pillows, on a bed in a room with a small gas fire burning. Her cheeks were flushed and her blue eyes open very wide, looking a little too brilliant as if she were running a temperature.

It was June-Patrushka.

Rollison waited for Mrs Mee to go while the girl stared at him without speaking. The door closed and Rollison approached the single bed standing against one wall of the room which was high enough only for that, a dressing-table and a small chair. Smiling crookedly and looking down at her, knowing that it was hardly fair to take advantage of her weakness and shock, Rollison dared not miss the opportunity of turning the situation to his advantage.

'Hallo, Patrushka,' he said. 'We both got wet.'

The way she started and moved back against the pillow at the name 'Patrushka' satisfied him that he had made a good start.

CHAPTER FIFTEEN

THE TRUTH, INSISTS ROLLISON

She did not ask how he had heard of the name but recovered a little from the first shock and raised a right hand from the bedspread; the shaded light glinted on the three diamonds of her engagement ring. He thought that her cheeks were flushed a little more than when he had first entered.

'You've been making inquiries, have you?'

'They seemed to be necessary,' said Rollison drily. 'And I'm not alone, Patrushka. The police are as interested and they'll be here before long to find out what they can about the attack on you. You haven't overlooked that, have you?'

'No,' she answered.

'And you haven't forgotten your fears of what will happen if they know that you're a Rumanian subject,' continued the Toff. 'Or has that obsession left you?' He paused but as she did not speak went on: 'Who told you that Patrushka was a Rumanian name?'

She said: 'Why, it—'

She stopped in confusion and this time there was no doubt that her cheeks were more flushed. That did not rob her of her attractiveness and, by some miracle, her hair was smooth about her head, fluffy because of the wetting but not greatly out of place. Her eyes looked enormous and her lips were parted a little, showing a glimpse of white teeth. She looked half-afraid of him.

'It isn't Rumanian, it's Russian,' said Rollison. 'Any Rumanian should know that. Patrushka, you lied convincingly to me this morning but I told you at the time that I wasn't deceived, although I was nearer to it than you thought. You're as English as I am. That covers the first direct lie you told me. Yes?'

She swallowed hard. 'I—'

'You wanted to give me a plausible reason for keeping free from the police while searching for the black case and, knowing through the Red Cross that aliens are always in trouble and likely to suffer a lot of inconvenience over here, you put that up as an excuse. It might have served but your English is a little too good, and you use colloquialisms too freely, to be really convincing. But as an alias for the benefit of Peveril you chose a name at random that sounded foreign and you thought it would serve your purpose. Perhaps it did but it didn't stop Lie Number 2 when you denied knowing Peveril.'

She said in a low-pitched voice:

'I had to tell you something.'

'Yes, I suppose so,' said the Toff. 'Tonight you're going to tell me the truth. Probably you'll just have time before the police arrive and I can help you with them if I'm sure that you've been frank with me. But if you try more evasions, I'll just give them my blessing and stand aside.'

He thought that she was scared of the prospect of police interrogation and he wanted her to be. But he was by no means certain that she would submit to his persuasion and could think of no yardstick by which he could measure her sincerity: her ability to tell a plausible story had been ably demonstrated that morning and he was in no condition to judge the truth of what she told him; that would be difficult enough in normal circumstances.

A tap on the door interrupted his thoughts.

Still glowing under the promise of compensation the angular Mrs Mee, who had powdered her face and dabbed a lipstick on her lips, brought in a tray on which were two large steaming cups of coffee. She was dressed in a black satin frock which rustled and crinkled, beamed upon them and put the tray on the dressing-table within easy reach of the bed.

'I thought you might change your mind, sir,' she said. 'You can't get too hot after what you've been through. And don't spare the sugar, don't be afraid of it.' Her beam widened, she was austerity unbending. 'What a lucky girl you are,' she added archly and shook a finger at Patrushka. 'If this brave gentleman hadn't jumped in after you, I wouldn't like to think what would have happened. Why, it's a wonder you wasn't froze to death as soon as you got in. Is there anything else you want, sir?'

'No, thanks,' said Rollison, who had borrowed cigarettes and matches from George on the strict understanding that he would replace them.

The girl lay back more easily on her pillows and there was a different expression in her eyes, thoughtful, considering and surprised. Rollison was about to speak again when Mrs Mee tapped again and entered quickly, her face set in lines of apology.

'I'm awfully sorry, sir, but a taxi-man downstairs says shall he wait, or shall he make a day of it? If you ask me, he's a bit worried

180

about his fare, some people *are* the limit.' She sniffed righteously.

'Yes, aren't they,' said Rollison. 'Tell him to wait, please, and that it will be worth a fiver.' He turned back to Patrushka without waiting to see the avaricious glint in Mrs Mee's eyes and heard the door close gently, accompanied by the exuding of a long, slow breath.

Patrushka completely ignored the interruption.

'I was the only one around,' said Rollison apologetically. 'And I wanted to talk with you, so there was nothing else to do.' His eyes were smiling but there was an underlying note of seriousness in his voice. 'What happened to you before you—er—fell in?'

'I didn't fall,' she said, and then abruptly: 'But you know that as well as I do. I—I went to sec the Jamesons but they were out.' She paused before going on: 'I have a key to the cottage and I went in. Some men were waiting for me—I think Ibbetson was among them.'

'He was,' confirmed the Toff.

'The brute,' she said and shuddered a little; it was not affectation. 'I don't know much more, except that they hit me over the head and I—I fainted. Before that I thought they seemed in a hurry to get me away. One of them said that there wasn't time to ask questions.' She stopped and leaned forward for her coffee. She wore a voluminous flannel nightdress, chastely drawn high at the neck

181

and with half-length sleeves from which her rounded forearm poked modestly. 'Thanks,' she added as Rollison handed her the cup and she took a spoonful of sugar. 'That's all I *do* remember about it.'

'I hope it is,' said Rollison.

'I'm telling you it is,' said Patrushka. 'I—I was in two minds whether to tell you all I can before that old bag of bones came in but now—well, I didn't realise that I owed you my life.'

'I suppose it is a point,' admitted Rollison.

'Well, my name *is* June Lancing, I am as English as you are and I lied to you this morning because I didn't want you to know what was happening. I thought you would be—be unable to get any further and that you'd just forget the affair. I knew you worked at the War Office, you see, and I thought you'd be too busy to give a lot of time to this.'

'I am busy,' Rollison assured her. 'This is a spare-time hobby.'

'It hasn't been today!' There was a hint of a smile on her lips and, in spite of the questions and the crisis which he had forced, the brilliance of her eyes and the flush of her cheeks seemed less pronounced. 'Oh, don't let's play on words, I'm tired of pretending. I've been pretending for so long. What do you want to know?'

'How did you know that I was involved?' asked the Toff promptly, and her answer was as quick.

'The Jamesons told me.'

'How did you come to know the Jamesons?'

'They worked for my father for a long time. That was before the war,' she added quietly. 'He died and mother and I gave up our big house and took a London flat. The Jamesons owned the cottage here, so they came to live in it. We—we gave them a pension, of course. Mr Roll—but what is your rank?'

'Mr will do.'

'I was going to say, this *is* the truth.'

'I'm not going to doubt where it can be checked easily,' said Rollison quietly and her cheeks flushed. But she went on without comment.

'They told us that you'd been at the cottage and old Jameson remembered about you. Tom followed your—your adventures when he was younger and I remembered something about you, so I asked a friend what he knew of you. As soon as I knew that you were all right, I sent the black case to your office for safety. That was last night. I thought it would be easy enough to get it back. I didn't know what was going to happen.'

'Not having second sight. So Lie Number 3 is that the case was stolen from you.'

'Oh, no,' the girl said quickly. 'It was stolen and then Peveril stole it from Ibbetson and I— well, I managed to get it back. I knew I dared not keep it for long, so I sent it to a Messenger

183

Service and told them to address it to you and take it to the War Office first thing in the morning. I didn't think there would be more than one Rollison working there and—well, it seemed safer than the flat.'

'Why?'

'Because I've realised how easily flats can be broken into,' the girl replied quietly. 'I thought I'd put it where it could come to no harm, this time. Then soon afterwards that brute Peveril forced his way into the flat. It—it was pretty bad for half an hour. He threatened some beastly things and I just couldn't stand out against him. Thank God he believed me!' she added and Rollison did not doubt her sincerity then. 'Doesn't he make the hair rise up on the back of your neck?'

'He hasn't yet,' said the Toff, 'but if you mean does he strike me as being a poisonous customer, yes. But you nearly qualified for the insanity stakes, you know. If you took the trouble to inquire about me why the deuce didn't you make a job of it and come to ask me to help?'

She said steadily: 'It would have meant telling you what was in the case. I couldn't do that.'

'The contents are as incriminating as that, are they?' asked Rollison quietly. 'What kind of a mess have you got yourself into, Patrushka? Who in the name of heaven persuaded you to try to handle it on your

184

own?'

After a long pause she said tensely:

'I had to work on my own, I couldn't consult anyone else, I didn't know where it would lead to. I didn't get the case from Mr Brett. I'm not engaged to his son.' Those admissions came abruptly. 'I told you both those things to make it sound more convincing.' Her voice dropped to a lower pitch, quivering a little, and the cup and saucer shook in her hand. 'I've told you that my father died and we had to give up the country house. That's true but he was murdered, I know he was murdered and the evidence is in that case. Brett killed him, I'm sure of it. He killed him and robbed the estate, he's like a great beast of prey, feeding on his victims. My father was one of a dozen, of a hundred! But Brett was too secure, no-one suspected the great Lancelot Brett of being a thief and a rogue and a swindler. Why, the Government consults him and entrusts him with its secrets; he's gone to America for them now; but if they knew the truth they wouldn't trust him an inch. I thought if I could get the case I could prove it. I know it holds all his secrets. My father told me he'd seen Brett consulting it. Don't look at me as if you don't believe me!' she flared up suddenly. 'It's true!'

She glared at him and a little of the coffee spilt into the saucer while the Toff leaned forward and touched her wrist, a soft, almost caressing gesture of reassurance. He smiled a little, intent only on easing her feeling, suddenly bubbling up and showing the pent-up emotions within her. That persuaded him more than anything else of her earnestness and her conviction.

'Yes, I believe you,' he said quietly. 'Don't get worked up, Patrushka, I'll see you through. And I'll look after him, too.' She gasped: 'Him? Who do you mean?'

'Whoever you're working for,' said Rollison gently. 'Whoever you're helping. The man who gave you that engagement ring, I imagine, and because of whom you daren't confide in the police and you didn't want to confide in me. There is a "him," isn't there?'

In a strangled voice she said:

'Yes, but—how did you know?'

'If all you've told me is true, and I think it is, you wanted to get the case open first, to extract something incriminating. Unless that was so you would have told the police at once or I'm no judge of Patrushka-June Lancing. Let it all come out now, even a half-truth or a single fact not disclosed might make all the difference between winning and losing.' Rollison talked to soothe her, using the first words that came into his mind, believing he had divined the truth and seeing confirmation in her eyes. He watched her closely, seeing her lips moving as her breathing quickened and her eyes, with their great lashes, wider open than he had ever seen them.

186

'Oh, dear God!' she exclaimed. 'I can't face it, I'm frightened he'll be found out. Oh, Gerry! Why did you have to do it, why couldn't you have fought against it?' She stopped, but her great eyes still stared at the Toff.

He sensed the depths of her emotion and forgot the questions crowding his mind in the revelation of a heart laid bare to him. To this girl the unknown 'Gerry' mattered more than anyone or anything in the world.

In a brittle voice she went on:

'Brett employed a secretary who knew almost as much as he did. Gerry killed him. The evidence is in the case. And I had it in my hands for hours. I had it in my hands but I daren't open it. I just daren't. I knew what would happen if I did. I could have destroyed it but it would have ruined the chances of bringing Brett's crimes home to him, as well as of freeing Gerry. I couldn't destroy it,' she went on tautly. 'I couldn't do that, I couldn't let such a man go free.'

Quietly, not then comprehending, Rollison said:

'Why couldn't you open it, Patrushka?'

He was not giving all his thought to what he said; he was thinking of the unknown Gerry to whom the contents of the case, if the girl were right, would bring home murder. He was thinking of the fact that Grice had the case and that there was little or no chance of examining the contents before the police did.

187

He was wondering what Patrushka would think and do when she knew that he had given it to the police, was reproaching himself for having let Grice have it although in his heart he knew that it had been the right thing to do. He was strangely disturbed by thought of Gerry; the tension in the girl explained that to some degree. He was disturbed, too, because of the likely effect of the revelation on her. He did not stop, then, to reason out the probable truth of Peveril's and Ibbetson's search for the case although his mind did admit the probability that, if it contained such information against Lancelot Brett, it would be a weapon of untold value in the hands of a blackmailer.

Many of the problems were settling themselves.

Subconsciously he realised that and, if he had not yet learned why a Commando had run amok or another man had pretended to, the threads were being disentangled, the worst confusion was in the human problem only then impressing itself on his mind.

The girl did not answer, and he repeated:

'Why couldn't you open it, Patrushka?'

'I—daren't,' she breathed. 'I hadn't the key and if it's forced it will explode and kill anyone within a dozen yards. Brett boasted about that; he didn't mean anyone to get that evidence. I had to get the key as well as the case.'

Then she stopped and it was her turn to see

dismay on Rollison's face. He stood staring at her, hard-eyed and with a cold hand gripping his vitals. He was thinking of Grice trying to force open the case.

CHAPTER SIXTEEN

'KEEP IT CLOSED'

'What is it?' demanded Patrushka. 'What's the matter?' As Rollison did not answer immediately, she leaned forward and stretched out a hand. 'Who has the case?' she breathed. 'Where is it?'

In spite of the sudden surge of fear for Grice and others at the Yard and the total unexpectedness of the news, Rollison did not mention the police. He turned to the door, reaching it in one stride across the tiny room, saying:

'Friends of mine are going to try to open it.'

'They mustn't do that!' cried the girl. 'It will be fatal, tell them to keep it closed!'

'Fatal in two ways, yes,' said Rollison. 'I'll be back.'

There was no light on the landing or downstairs in the little hall and he stumbled on the first stair, slipping but saving himself from falling by clutching the handrail. He made noise enough to make June Lancing call out in anxious inquiry and for light to shine suddenly as a door opened below. Mrs Mee's voice came upwards urgently:

'Who's that. What's happening?'

Rollison went down the rest of the stairs swiftly, calling as he went.

'Where's the nearest telephone. Is it far away?'

'There's a kee-osk outside Green's, the butcher's,' Mrs Mee told him, staring at his strained face. 'You can get there in ten minutes, sir.'

'Too far,' said Rollison briefly. 'Isn't there one at a private house?' He had the front door open by then and the woman hurried agitatedly towards him.

'Oh, sir, please mind the blackout, they make a fuss.' She pushed the door to firmly and then went on: 'Mr Yateman has got one, but he's a miserable old—I mean he doesn't like the neighbours using it.'

'I'm not a neighbour,' retorted Rollison. 'Where is his house? This is urgent,' he added sharply as he pulled at the door.

His manner more than his words made her allow the door to open although light streamed into the street. Hurriedly she told him that Mr Yateman lived two doors along on the same side of the road, that he was rather deaf.

Rollison reached the small gate before he paused. In his anxiety to get word to Grice he

190

had overlooked the possibility that the girl might decide to take to flight again now that she had said so much. The approach of a dark figure in policeman's uniform helped to solve the difficulty.

'Put that light out,' began the constable and the door closed abruptly.

Rollison spoke on the man's words, without preamble.

'Go in there, constable and make sure that the young lady upstairs stays in her room—Mrs Mee will tell you which young lady. I'm speaking for Superintendent Grice,' he added, then pushed past the policeman and reached the gate of the second house away. Visions of waiting and fuming on the doorstep faded for the door was opened quickly upon his ring; the faintest of faint lights showed a little man in silhouette.

'May I use your telephone, please,' said Rollison, and added the *open sesame*. 'Police business.'

'Eh?' said the little man, barring his path.

So he was deaf, thought Rollison and drew a deep breath preparatory to shouting, then thought better of it and leaned forward, putting his lips close to the man's right ear.

'Telephone—urgent,' he said clearly.

'Oh, no you don't,' said the deaf Mr Yateman. 'I won't be bothered by being called at this time of night to let people use the telephone.

191

'*Police*!' declared Rollison harshly.

'Police!' echoed Mr Yateman, backing a pace. 'Oh, I see. Well, I suppose you'd better use it, then. Close the door,' he added, complainingly, 'you'll need the light on, I suppose.'

He indicated the instrument in the hall and the Toff dialled Whitehall 1212, getting no immediate connection and fuming at the delay. When he thought dispassionately he considered the probability that Grice had already made the effort and, if Brett's declaration to the girl about the case were true, then there was little hope for the Superintendent or those who had been with him. Such a disaster would be too great and unexpected; the Toff found it inconceivable but the *brr-brr* of the ringing tone and the long time that it took for the answer made him fear that disaster had befallen the Yard. Surely there could be no other reasonable explanation of the delay? He dialled again, as Yateman made a *tcha-tcha* noise with his lips and then a cool voice announced:

'Scotland Yard speaking, can I help you?'

'It's Richard Rollison here,' said the Toff quickly, his forehead cold with perspiration. 'Get every line you can working for a call for Superintendent Grice. Tell him that Rollison says that the black case must be kept closed until I've seen him. It must be. Is that clear?'

'Black case, sir?' queried the operator.

192

'The little black one that I gave him.'

'I'll do what you ask at once, sir. Will you hold on?'

'I will,' said Rollison, oblivious to further *tcha-tchas* from Yateman and also to the fact that he retained the blanket which was about his shoulders and also dangling to his feet, likely to trip him if he moved again. A clock struck half-past eight; and the waiting seemed interminable.

* * *

That the case remained unopened as late as eight o'clock that evening was against all Grice's inclinations. It would have been forced at a much earlier hour had it not offered difficulties which Grice himself had found insuperable. He had sent for Sergeant MacAdam whose speciality was the opening of recalcitrant locks and the dismantling of complicated mechanisms. The sergeant soon admitted himself temporarily beaten and asked permission to take it to his workroom.

'I'll come with you,' Grice said.

That had been at three o'clock in the afternoon when the paper on and about the case had been thoroughly tested for fingerprints; it had yielded several, one set of a woman's fingers. Another set of prints belonged to a certain Charley Day who had a lengthy police record, always associated with

193

crimes of moderate violence.

A call had been put out for Charley Day immediately.

Then other news had come in.

Grice, a reasonable man in most things, did not want the case opened except in his presence and, when he heard of the murder at Victoria and the message from Rollison, he went to the apartment house himself, leaving instructions for work on the black case to be suspended. At Victoria he found the local police coping with Peveril who was insisting that he had urgent business and must be off at once. His blustering served only to stiffen Grice's manner and the Superintendent told Peveril acidly that he would be allowed to go only when the police were satisfied that he knew nothing of the murder; meanwhile his flat would be searched.

Peveril raved and stormed and finally lost his self-control enough to aim a blow at a sergeant. Grice snapped:

'That's more than enough. Take him to Cannon Row, sergeant, charged with attempting to impede the police in the course of their duty.'

The self-styled solicitor was led away, becoming so violent that he was handcuffed before being put into a taxi and taken to the police cells in the station adjoining Scotland Yard. Grice did not set too much store by the show of violence but gave his men instructions to search the two-roomed apartment carefully, even to raising the carpets and examining the floorboards. While that was being done, photographers and fingerprint men were busy in the bathroom and the doors of the other apartments while Grice had a short session with the police-surgeon.

During those diversions, Grice completely forgot the black case but the nimble-fingered MacAdam, who had it on the bench, kept glancing at the clock and hoping that Old Gricey would not be long; the case presented a challenge which the sergeant was anxious to take up. He even went so far as to finger it once or twice and peer at the tiny slit which appeared to be all that there was for a lock. He put it down when a colleague came in with a watch battered after a case of robbery with violence; the watch had to be taken to pieces and so the case lay untouched.

Grice was longer at Peveril's apartment than he expected and did not get away until nearly six o'clock. He went to Gresham Terrace but Rollison had left.

The only things found in Peveril's bureau that proved of interest were some photographs with names beneath them: amongst them was an old, nearly bald, thin-faced but handsome man, familiar to many economists and business experts as Lancelot Brett. Another was a partner of Brett in several business enterprises, Sir Gregory Lancaster. A third was of a fair-haired man in uniform, smiling and looking very different from Lancelot Brett, although he was Brett's son, Lionel. A fourth was of a girl, a personable-looking girl, who was named—on the photograph—'Patrushka Tonesco.' Grice frowned at that and stared hard for Tonesco was a Rumanian name and he had an obsession about aliens: he wondered why the Russian 'Patrushka' should be allied to 'Tonesco' and then passed on to the next photograph, one of Jacob Ibbetson. He looked plump, smiling, the picture of a good-natured and amiable man of the world. There were other photographs and Grice selected one of them and nodded slowly.

'Found something, sir?' asked the sergeant with him at the Yard where he was going through Peveril's effects before interviewing the man.

'Isn't that the dead man?' asked Grice and held up a head-and-shoulders photograph of Fred who had died in the bath. The sergeant nodded, frowned and reflected.

'Mr Rollison said that Peveril was with him all the time, didn't he?'

'Ye-es,' said Grice reluctantly.

'Of course, sir, Mr Rollison has been known to make misleading statements, hasn't he?'

'Has he?' asked Grice, non-committally and passed on to the next and last photograph. A fair-headed, youngish man in lounge clothes, good looking and yet by no means handsome,

196

with a smile which leapt out of the photograph and seemed to make a personal appearance in the Superintendent's roomy office, peered up silently at Grice.

'Nice-looking boy,' said the sergeant, breathing heavily down Grice's neck. 'Isn't he, sir?'

'Yes,' admitted Grice and read aloud from beneath the photograph: 'Gerald Paterson. H'm. Take these, sergeant, and check them all in Records. Bring me any papers we may have about any of them. Not that I expect a lot.'

'Are you going to see Peveril now, sir?'

'Shortly,' said Grice. 'I'll be in MacAdam's room if I'm wanted in the next half-hour. Ring the canteen and ask them to send me a cup of tea and some sandwiches there, will you?'

He went eagerly upstairs to MacAdam's workshop to find the man, with a watch-glass screwed into his right eye, bending over a jewelled timepiece.

'Wait a minute,' said MacAdam without looking up. Then: 'Who is it? Oh, sorry, sir.' He put the watch down hastily and the glass dropped from his eye, to be caught expertly. 'Come to have another go at the case, sir?'

'That's right,' said Grice.

'I've had a look at her,' confessed the expert. 'A beautiful job. I've never seen anything quite like it but I'll have it opened before I'm finished.' He picked up the black case and some delicate-looking instruments,

197

more befitting a surgeon's case than a mechanic's outfit, and began to work. He concentrated for fifteen minutes while Grice had tea and sandwiches; by then it was nearly seven o'clock.

The telephone rang at seven with a summons from the Assistant Commissioner who wanted to see the Superintendent immediately. Grice scowled and MacAdam looked hopefully at him.

'Shall I carry on with it, sir?'

'No,' said Grice, slowly and obstinately. 'I won't be long. Wait for me, Mac, will you?' He went out, aware of MacAdam's darkling thoughts but in no way perturbed by them, and hurried to the AC's office. There he gave a full report on the Jameson case: even Grice had almost forgotten that Jameson had been in since early in the affair which had started from an attempted mass murder in Chiswick.

The AC kept him nearly an hour: he was finishing the interview when Rollison was being given hot coffee in the house next door to Mrs Mee, just before going to the girl. Grice was frowning when he left the AC, who asked for more results and questioned the wisdom of letting Rollison do just what he wanted. Then he turned his footsteps eagerly towards the workroom, anxious to get busy on the box which was defying MacAdam's efforts so stoutly but which MacAdam would certainly contrive to open sooner or later.

He was at the door of the workroom when a man called:

'Mr Grice—excuse me, sir, there's some news about the Jameson case.'

'What is it?' Grice asked swiftly.

He received a report, none of it very clear, on something of what had happened near Canal Cottage. Rollison's part was not emphasised, although it was made clear that Rollison had been perilously close to being drowned, together with a girl so far unnamed. Grice played with the idea of going to Wembley at once but decided that he would be wise to interrogate Peveril and to get the case open before seeing or worrying further about the Toff. Nevertheless, he was pre-occupied when he rejoined MacAdam who picked up the case eagerly.

The sergeant was past wondering why Old Gricey was so anxious to be present when the little case was opened but took it for granted that it would contain something of particular importance.

MacAdam was a man running to flesh, of medium height, middle-aged and with a small bald patch on a head surrounded by frizzy, grey hair. His round face was almost cherubic and he was deservedly popular at the Yard.

He began work again intently.

The case continued to baffle him but he did not lose patience and Grice felt only slightly exasperated. Neither of them dreamed of what was happening at Wembley, nor of the conversation between Rollison and the girl. None of them knew that as MacAdam eased back from the case and wiped his forehead, the girl was saying:

'*I daren't . . . if it's forced it will explode and kill anyone within a dozen yards.*'

'Getting any nearer?' asked Grice quietly.

'It *can't* take much longer,' declared MacAdam. 'I think I'm pretty well there now, sir.'

There was a tap on the door and a uniformed sergeant put his head round.

'Is Mr Grice there . . . oh, good evening, sir. We've just brought in Charley Day, picked him up at Willesden. He's waiting downstairs, sir. Shall I take him into your office?'

Grice frowned.

'No, I—what's he like?'

'I don't think he'll take much to crack, sir. He's heard that one of his pals has been croaked and he's pretty well ready to talk.' The sergeant paused and then dared to offer advice: 'He might close up if he's left too long, sir; he's the kind that does. Of course, I don't mean to suggest that—'

'All right, I'll come,' said Grice irritably.

MacAdam turned his cherubic face towards the Superintendent, a picture so forlorn that Grice could not resist a smile. In MacAdam's right hand there was a small tool, in the other he held the little black case.

200

'May I just finish *this* try, sir?'

'Oh, get the confounded thing open but don't touch the contents until I'm back,' said Grice. 'Ring me when you've had some luck.'

'Right-ho, sir, thanks!' exclaimed MacAdam gratefully and began again before the door closed.

Grice went downstairs to his office and waited for Charley Day. He had in front of him the photographs of Ibbetson and Charley, Fred and the other man, whom he did not know was called Mike, when the door opened and Charley was led in.

It was an ordeal for a man with a guilty conscience to come face to face with Superintendent Grice. On such occasions, Grice's face was cold and aloof; his taut skin seemed to shine and his eyes appeared to probe beneath the surface of his victim's mind, making it seem that there was no chance of getting away with a lie or even a half-truth. And Charley Day was in bad shape. His hands and lips were trembling and his clothes were dishevelled for he had tried to evade arrest before being handcuffed by the Willesden Police.

It was no fault of the Willesden authorities that they did not know that Day had been on the way to The Bargee, near the canal.

'I want to talk to you, Day,' began Grice coldly. 'And I mean to have the truth from you. This is a murder case and there'll be no fooling.'

'Murder,' muttered Charley, white to the lips. 'I never did it, I never—'

He stopped abruptly and Grice and the sergeant with him stared towards the door which rattled against the blast from an explosion not far away. The boom echoed about that wing of the Yard, the sound of breaking glass and falling debris followed and immediately upon it there were hurrying footsteps.

'That—that was a bomb!' gasped Charley. 'Where's the shelter, where's the shelter? They've come again!'

Grice turned back to the man.

'If there's any danger we'll go to a shelter but not before.'

But he was not allowed to go on for the door burst open and two men entered, one an Inspector, the other a uniformed constable. The Inspector spoke first, staring at Grice and looking both excited and disturbed.

'Did you hear that?'

'It was a bomb—' began Charley.

'Bomb my foot!' exclaimed the Inspector. 'That came from upstairs. I've just tried to get on to the next floor. The staircase is choked up with debris and there's a fire starting. You can't see anything of Mac's workshop. What's he been up to, do you know?'

Grice said nothing but stared for a moment before abruptly pushing his chair back.

CHAPTER SEVENTEEN

EVERYTHING GONE?

'Hallo,' said Rollison urgently. 'Hallo, operator, are you there?' He spoke thus, not because of Yateman scowling a little way along the passage but because he found the waiting intolerable. If Grice were at the Yard he should have reached the phone a long while before but since the operator had promised to ring every line for him there had been no response.

'Hallo!' exclaimed Rollison again. 'Are you—?'

'Are you there, sir?' asked the Yard operator quietly. 'Mr Grice is coming, he won't be a moment.'

'He—oh, thanks,' said Rollison. He wiped his hand across his damp forehead. 'He's all right?'

'*He's* all right, sir,' the man assured him and Rollison missed the emphasis on the pronoun in relief at the knowledge that Grice was unhurt. He waited for at least another minute, then heard the Superintendent's crisp voice:

'Well, Rollison, what have you been up to?'

'Never mind that,' snapped Rollison. 'Did you get my message? Did the operator tell you to leave the case alone at all costs?'

203

'I had the message just now,' Grice said soberly. 'It was too late.'

'Too late?' echoed Rollison and drew a deep breath. Nothing in Grice's tone suggested that there was disaster to relate and he saw a picture of June Lancing, sitting up in bed with the voluminous flannel nightdress about her, telling him that if the case were forced, anyone within a dozen yards would be killed. 'D'you mean you've managed to get it open?'

'I don't know,' said Grice.

He told the Toff just what had happened; and he named MacAdam, whom the Toff had known well and had liked. The news was a shock despite the fact that, since Grice was safe, it came as something of an anticlimax. Rollison felt subdued, relieved that the girl had at least told the truth but deploring the fact that she had delayed it for so long. He did not find the heart to blame her for that: he should have told her the moment he had seen her that the police were going to open the case.

'Are you there?' asked Grice, after a pause.

'Yes,' said the Toff. 'Yes, I'm terribly sorry. How long ago?'

'Not more than half an hour,' said Grice. 'How did you know what would happen?'

'I'll tell you later,' said the Toff slowly. 'You've heard about the other bother here, I suppose? And you're looking for Ibbetson now?'

'Thanks for permitting it,' said Grice sardonically.

'No, don't be clever,' implored the Toff. 'Neither of us have much to boast about in the show yet. But I've cleared up some odds and ends and I'll pass them on as soon as I can. What about Peveril?'

'He's at Cannon Row.'

'You haven't charged him with the murder?'

'Not yet,' said Grice. 'He's been violent and we've charged him with the usual hocus pocus. We'll look after Peveril, don't worry. But it's time you and I really came to an understanding,' continued Grice. 'Can you come here at once?'

Rollison answered slowly:

'Not quite at once but I'll be there as soon as I can. There are bits and pieces I can look after here, first. I won't be a minute longer than I can help.'

He replaced the receiver, wiped his forehead again then turned towards the door, his only thought the need for returning to June and telling her what had happened for she had to know. The shock of the news would probably be enough to loosen her tongue and make her talk freely.

'*Here!*' ejaculated Yateman loudly. 'What do you think *you're* doing?'

He grabbed Rollison's elbow and pushed an open palm forward; Rollison stared at him, at a loss, then realised that the man was asking for the coppers for the call. He drew a deep breath, sought in the pockets of the borrowed suit and found them empty. He nearly lost his patience with the little man, who insisted on accompanying him to Mrs Mee's, where he borrowed precisely tuppence and dropped the two coppers into Yateman's outstretched hand.

'And thank you very much for your courtesy,' he said ironically as Yateman turned and left the hall of his neighbour.

'How would you like to have to live in the same street as 'im?' breathed Mrs Mee. She glowered at the door, showing what she thought of Yateman and then lowered her voice and raised her eyebrows, contriving also to point upwards towards the landing. 'The policeman's there; is it okay?'

'Yes,' said Rollison. 'I wanted to make sure that the young lady was all right. She's been attacked once this evening, you know.'

'Attacked!' breathed Mrs Mee. 'Attacked! What for?'

The question startled the Toff who had to admit that he did not know the answer. He went upstairs, followed by Mrs Mee's avaricious, but wondering, eyes. He nodded to the constable who had so faithfully obeyed him, tapped on the door and entered the girl's room.

He thought at first glimpse that she was

asleep.

Then she opened her eyes and stared at him. She was lying down in the bed and her hair was a dark flurry about the pillows; it reminded him of the way it had looked when it had floated on the surface of the canal. Her cheeks were pale, her eyes lack-lustre. As he reached the end of the bed she struggled up to a sitting position.

'Well?'

'What do you expect?' asked Rollison, finding it hard to speak normally and seeing a picture of MacAdam's frizzy hair in his mind's eye. It merged with the girl's and became a part of it, a disturbing thing.

'Did—did your friends try to open it?' she asked.

Rollison sat at the foot of the bed and said deliberately:

'My friends were the police. They did try to open it. At least one was killed, others may have been. If the truth had been known about that case earlier, this could have been prevented.'

He needed to shape no words of accusation, the implication was sufficient. June kept quite still, colour gradually suffusing her face and in her eyes appeared a reflection of horror which made Rollison wonder whether the cruelty of his abruptness had been necessary.

'You shouldn't have given it to them.'

'We won't have exercises in passing the

buck,' said the Toff thinly. 'We'll just face up to the position as it is. If you're right, any evidence existing against Brett and against your Gerald has been destroyed.'

'Is—is *everything* gone?' she whispered.

'From all accounts, yes.'

He would not have been surprised had she shown some degree of relief because of what it meant to Gerry but her expression did not grow easier; he imagined that she was thinking of the man who had been killed; but it was not altogether that, for she said after a long pause:

'So Brett will get away with it?'

'Has he done anything to get away with?' demanded the Toff, 'or have you pitched another fine story?'

'Oh, you fool!' stormed the girl. 'Oh, you poor fool! Of course he's guilty of a hundred crimes: he ought to be hanged, he ought to spend the rest of his life in prison. And now no one will be able to bring it home to him, no one. And—Gerry,' she added, and her voice was a sigh. 'Poor Gerry.'

'I think it's time I knew a little more about Gerry,' said Rollison and then went on in a kindlier tone: 'June, we must face up to the position, we can't hedge. The police will want to know everything you can tell them and you'll have to explain your interest in the case. The only effective way will be by naming Gerry.'

'I can't do that.'

'You must,' insisted Rollison.

'I can't, I won't! I—but you'll tell them.' She broke off. 'You'll tell them. Oh, what a fool I was to say anything to you. Why couldn't I keep my silly mouth closed? I won't say anything more,' she added desperately. 'It's no use trying to make me!'

'If you don't, the police will detain you.'

'I don't care about that.'

'You'll come to care,' the Toff assured her quietly. 'June, have you realised what this means to you? And do you really think that there's the slightest chance of keeping anything from the police for long? They'll ferret it all out and, when the truth is known and they realise that you could have helped them and saved a great deal of trouble, they'll believe there's a much more involved and discreditable explanation than the one you'll give. The police are materialistic and hard-hearted. They don't believe in gallantry and quixoticism for the sake of it. Crime is sordid in their experience and they'll work on the assumption that this case is, too. You'll do your Gerry more harm than good by keeping silent and you'll do yourself untold harm. Be sensible, and tell everything.'

'No!'

Rollison shrugged his shoulders, stood up and took a cigarette from the borrowed packet. He lit it and flicked the match to the little surround of the gas fire.

'Well, please yourself. It isn't the first time I've found a girl throwing herself away on a useless wastrel but I don't enjoy the experience any more each time it happens.'

Her eyes flashed. 'What do you mean?'

'If there's any kind of manhood in Gerry he won't let it happen,' said the Toff evenly. 'It isn't a habit that a decent man develops, you know. It's called hiding behind a woman's skirts and it's frowned upon.'

'Oh, you fool,' she flung at him. 'He doesn't know.'

'So you'll defend him at all costs,' said Rollison with a contemptuous gesture.

'He doesn't know, I tell you! He's in the RAF up in Yorkshire and he hasn't been down here for months. If only you knew what he's been through! I know that he often wishes he would get shot down when he goes out on raids, he's always taking chances, he—he's even got two bars to the DFC. For years Biett has been torturing him, blackmailing him, it's cost him tens of thousands. Now he's nearly a pauper, he hasn't much more than his RAF pay to live on. If he knew what was happening he'd get down here somehow but I was praying that I'd be able to get the case and take his papers out before—before he knew anything about it. He mustn't know what I've been doing!' she repeated wildly. 'You can't tell him, you wouldn't be such a brute!'

She had a queerly effective way of

touching him, Rollison thought only half-dispassionately; she put such emotion into her words and, while he could not be sure that she was telling the truth, he contrasted her manner now with that of the morning when she had been indifferent, aloof, completely self-reliant. If there were such a man as Gerry, he was in at least one way a lucky man. If only he, the Toff, could be sure of the truth of what she told him, it would help.

'Now listen, June,' he said paternally. 'I can imagine how you feel but getting excited won't help you. You aren't being sensible, you know, and—'

'Sensible!'

'It always pays,' the Toff assured her. 'Ibbetson is being sought all over the country, as well as his men, one of whom has been murdered. That means that the police won't let anything rest; when it's a case of murder they go all out and there isn't a chance of standing out against them. Peveril has been arrested on suspicion of the murder and he isn't a man who will keep silent for long. One or the other of them knows about your Gerry and if you don't talk, they will. Get in on the ground floor and show some faith both in Gerry and in getting a fair deal from the authorities.

'But he killed a man,' she exclaimed.

'Who had been blackmailing him or helping to.'

'What difference does that make?'

'Extreme provocation is a strong plea in court,' Rollison assured her. 'You tell me that Gerry has been and is being blackmailed by Brett and that he hasn't a penny to bless himself with, that he's flying without any real heart and hopes that he'll be brought down. What kind of a life is that? If he did commit murder in the face of extreme provocation, and proof against Brett and his late secretary will be reasonable proof of the provocation, it isn't likely that he'll be found guilty of murder. I don't know the circumstances but I've known murder charges reduced to manslaughter because the police see the strength of the provocation and know that no jury will bring in a verdict of guilty on a murder charge. I've known lawyers get the accused off scot free with a defence of justifiable homicide. And I've also known the lives of men and women ruined completely by a refusal to come into the open.

'Don't keep this to yourself any longer,' Rollison went on. 'Bring it out and fight all you know. If you've told me the truth now and Gerry can prove that he was more sinned against than sinning, I'll help you all I can and I'll brief the best men in the country for you. Money needn't be an obstacle. The only obstacle is obstinacy and a belief that there'll be disaster if you tell the truth. There won't. The only chance you've got of getting out of

212

this with any degree of happiness for either of you is to tell everything to the police. I'm not persuading you for the sake of a cheap success,' Rollison added quietly. 'I mean all I'm saying and if you do the wise thing I know you'll feel a hundred times happier in the morning than you do now.'

He paused and waited, seeing the uncertainty in her eyes. He did not seriously doubt that she felt for Gerry as deeply as she declared: he believed that she had come to the end of prevarication and smoothly-told plausible stories. Quietly he went on:

'If you tell me everything else now, I'll pass it on to the police so that you're not worried tonight or until you feel better. And don't think that, because the black case has been destroyed, all the evidence has gone completely. Your evidence and Gerry's will be strong enough to enable the police to start working against Brett and, once they start, they'll uncover the rest. You've told me that Brett has hundreds of victims. You might be the source of saving them all from further torment and further suffering. If you're right, if Brett is the rogue you've made out, then the right thing to do is to fight to prove it.'

When he stopped, the room was very quiet. She did not close her eyes but stared at him expressionlessly, the colour gone from her cheeks again, her eyes lack-lustre. He saw that her hands were clenched over the bedspread

213

and thought that she was grinding her teeth. He fought against a temptation to add more persuasion, waiting for a long time without moving.

Then she said very slowly:

'Will—will you tell Gerry what you're going to do, first? If I give you his name, will you promise me that?'

'Yes,' said Rollison unhesitatingly.

'All right,' she said. 'All right. I expect you're wise, it's been a dreadful time. But Gerry—I don't know what he'll say. I don't know whether he'll think it's worth it.'

'He will,' the Toff assured her, with quiet assurance. 'He'll see the sense of it, June, and he'll see the chance of laying a ghost. Now, what's his full name, his station and the name of his CO, if you know it?'

She told him that he was Gerald Paterson and gave him the other information. She also solved a problem that had been worrying him; the man who had taken her from her work in a car was a neighbour and always gave her a lift. She seemed listless and very tired when he finished and he believed that the effort, the shock and the fierceness of her fight against him had completed the effect of the immersion and exposure; now she would sleep. While she slept he had much to do.

CHAPTER EIGHTEEN

FLIGHT TO THE NORTH

Pondering the girl's reaction after her decision, Rollison left the room, not surprised to find Mrs Mee in an upstairs room; the light there was on and he caught a glimpse of the woman's back, assuming that she had been doing all she could to eavesdrop. He made no comment but said quietly:

'Didn't the doctor advise a sleeping draught?'

'Why, yes, sir. I put it in her coffee.'

'Oh,' said Rollison, relieved that the draught was causing June's apparent listlessness but startled because she might have submitted to its influence before he had gained the information. 'That's good. I'm going next door to see whether my uniform is dry yet. There'll be a policeman on duty in the house all night, I'm afraid.'

'Lawks!' exclaimed Mrs Mee. 'I've *never* 'ad—but if it's to help the young lady, sir, that's all right, o'course it's quite all right.'

'Good, thanks,' said Rollison. 'I'll see you again tomorrow.'

The uniformed man was standing in the porch and Rollison exchanged a few words with him, to be interrupted by the sergeant who had transmitted his earlier message to Grice. The sergeant had instructions, it seemed, to make sure that no one involved in the canal incident was allowed to escape police observation, although Mr Rollison had not been included in that general order. The sergeant, therefore, promised to see that the girl was watched and then said:

'I inquired for Mr Jolly, sir.'

'Yes?' Rollison's voice grew sharp.

'He was there,' said the sergeant and Rollison's fears abated. 'I sent one of my men who isn't well known, sir, and pretended that there was a message waiting for him at his home.' The constable smiled although the darkness hid the fact from Rollison. 'Mr Jolly took it up very quickly and mentioned casually he had only just managed to rent a flat nearby, so I don't think anyone thought much about it.'

'Good,' said the Toff. 'Where is Jolly?'

'Still at the pub, sir. He asked me to tell you that he thought it would be worth staying there for an hour; he got talking to several people who were there when young Jameson got tight the other night.'

'I see,' said the Toff slowly. 'That should work out all right. What kind of reputation has The Bargee got?'

'Not a mucher,' he was assured. 'They're a funny crowd that rents it but they do good business. I've left a man outside, just in case of

216

accidents. From what the Superintendent told me this is going to be some case and if it's connected with what that young Jameson's charged with that's not far out.'

'Did you know Jameson?'

'Oh, yes, sir, fairly well. He hasn't lived 'ere long but he was a nice young fellow; the last thing I could have expected was for him to get a brainstorm and do anything like *that*.' On the 'that' he lowered his voice and then went on: 'Will one man be enough at the pub, do you think?'

'I'd make it three at least,' said the Toff. 'Oh, sergeant. When you've strengthened the watch there, telephone Mr Grice for me, will you? Tell him that I've had to go north in a hurry but that I hope to be back tomorrow with some news of importance.'

The sergeant assured him that he would do that at once and Rollison returned to the first house. The plump little woman, so much more genuinely hospitable than Mrs Mee, assured him that she would not dream of letting him have his uniform: he would catch his death if he put it on. Wouldn't he stay the night? She could easily make up a bed and he'd be much better for it.

'Thanks very much,' smiled Rollison, 'but I must go now. I'll come and see you again,' he added, before saying *au revoir* to George and the others who had played a part in the rescue and going into the blackout to find the taxi driver waiting patiently.

'It's a bit nippy aht 'ere, sir, ain't it? Where to?'

Rollison went to his flat, donned a fresh uniform and then was driven to the Whitehall building. He dismissed the cabby with a fiver and, with the man's warm thanks echoing in his ears, went up to the office.

The night staff in some departments were on duty and he telephoned a colleague who acted as liaison officer between his department and its equivalent at the Air Ministry. The liaison officer was on duty and led off by saying that he thought Rollison was taking French Leave.

'Only more or less,' said the Toff. 'Tim, if you can perform miracles, here's one waiting for you. I want a man, at the Bedloe Station in Yorkshire, stopped from operational duty tonight if he's briefed for it and released to come down for a few days on urgent private matters.'

'*What?*' exclaimed Tim.

'Also, I want to get up to Bedloe to see him tonight,' continued the Toff. 'There's bound to be a 'plane going north with something on and it won't make a lot of difference if I'm dropped at Bedloe. Can you do it?'

'Of course I can't,' said Tim, and abruptly: 'What's the urgent private matter? Life and death?'

'Yes,' said the Toff emphatically.

218

'Hm. I *might* get him released,' said Tim. 'I know one or two men who'll pull what wires they can but I can't guarantee anything. And I certainly can't get you a seat on a 'plane going north. Damn it, man, do you know what you're asking?'

'Yes, and I'm not joking,' said Rollison quietly. 'You can arrange it if you exert yourself. I don't want to waste time going further upstairs.'

'I'll see what I can do,' said Tim gruffly. 'I'll ring you back.'

He rang off and Rollison pushed the telephone away and contemplated the files in which the day's correspondence was locked. He was not thinking of the correspondence but his justification in having reached a compromise with June and also for trying to get to see Gerald Paterson by air. Strictly speaking there was no justification for the latter and he was using his official position for essentially private purposes. It did not weigh on him heavily for he believed a talk with Paterson would do much to help him assess the situation. He was troubled, too, because earlier in the case an RAF officer had been mentioned. He could not remember in what connection.

The telephone rang as he was pondering the position so far reached and he did not think Tim could have made contact with the Air Ministry so quickly. Nevertheless it was Tim who said gruffly:

'Is that you, Rolly?'

'What's the bother?' asked the Toff.

'Just what *is* this show about?' demanded Tim. 'I'm bound to be asked.'

'It's an official request from me,' said Rollison, burning his boats completely, 'and it's on official business.' That at all events was a half-truth, if police counted as officials, and he added: 'I'll answer any questions that are put to me but for the love of Pete get going quickly; an hour might make the difference between life and death.'

He put that touch in for the sake of impressing Tim and not because he believed that it would make much difference—except to the peace of mind of a girl and possibly Paterson. He did not know that from a house in London, where Ibbetson had made a detailed report to his employer, two men had started out by road with instructions to persuade Gerry Paterson to leave Bedloe at once to come to London.

*   *   *

'All you want is to get Paterson off the aerodrome,' the man told them. 'You can't handle him when he's there but you can soon get at him when he's on the road. It doesn't matter how you do it but get rid of him.'

'Just *why* are you worried by Paterson?' he

was asked.

'Because his blasted girl and Rollison are together and Rollison will get the story from her,' said the man who had ordered the journey. 'Rollison and Paterson mustn't meet, d'you understand? It's as much as our lives are worth. They mustn't meet and Paterson mustn't be interviewed by the police. He's close to breaking point and he might break down into talking too freely. Get off and hurry. Make a good job of it.'

'And then what?' one of the men demanded.

'It will soon be over,' he was assured. 'You won't have to worry afterwards but get rid of Paterson and don't waste time.'

So the two men started for Bedloe in the blackout and were three hours on their way when Rollison sat at his desk and waited for the telephone call from Tim. To while away the time he unlocked the 'Correspondence Awaiting Reply' drawer of a cabinet and glanced through it. Several letters had been set aside for his personal attention and he pencilled notes on them. Half an hour passed but did not drag too slowly, although it would have seemed much longer had he known of the car forging along steadily just beyond Northampton on the road to York. He had finished a scribbled note when the telephone rang and Tim's voice sounded eagerly in his ear.

'You've the devil's own luck, Rolly. I've

221

fixed one part. You can go but Paterson's on ops tonight already.'

'Bless your little heart!' exclaimed the Toff. 'How soon do I start?'

'There's a car leaving the Air Ministry in twenty minutes,' said Tim. 'It'll take you to Hendon and there's a 'plane leaving for Lettley as soon as the car arrives. Carrying some papers,' Tim added briefly, 'and there's plenty of room. You'll have a Wing Commander with you and he might be curious. Don't let me down.'

Rollison smiled into the mouthpiece.

'I'll see you all right,' he said with assurance. 'One day I'll let you know what it's all about and you'll be glad you spread yourself. Cheerio.'

He replaced the receiver, bundled the file back into the cabinet and locked it and hurried downstairs. He was at the main doors of the Air Ministry building just fifteen minutes later; the sidelights of a car glowed eerily through the gloom and he approached the driver, a girl in uniform just visible in the reflected light.

'I think you're expecting me,' he said. 'Colonel Rollison.'

'The others won't be a moment, sir,' said the girl.

They followed almost on her words and with Rollison climbed into the tonneau. Rollison was brief but heartfelt in his thanks, a gruff-voiced man waived them and the journey to Hendon passed with neither incident nor comment. The transfer to the aeroplane, a twin engined bomber, was quickly accomplished and they took off within a few minutes of arriving at the airfield.

Once in the air, the gruff-voiced man said: 'Well, I'm going to have a nap. Need it.'

Obviously the machine had been converted for the seats were upholstered and the passengers' comfort well looked after. Faint snoring came in place of the gruff voice and the other man said little, evincing no curiosity whatsoever about the reason for an Army man's sudden journey. Rollison smiled appreciatively in the darkness and then settled down with the roar of the twin engines loud in his ears. Now and again a member of the crew passed him and, on the starboard side some half an hour along the journey, he saw a network of searchlights and coloured shells rising into the air. He even caught a glimpse of a machine illuminated by the searchlights with a dozen puffs of whitish smoke bursting about it. Then the silvery streak disappeared while his aircraft went onwards steadily.

The flight to Lettley took precisely two hours.

The gruff voice grunted once or twice after being awakened and they climbed from the 'plane to the landing ground. Rollison felt somewhat ill at ease as he asked one of his companions how far it was to Bedloe.

'Fifteen miles or so,' he was told. 'They may have a car going over there in the next hour. Hold on, I'll see.'

There was a car leaving at 3am, he was told a few minutes afterwards, which meant he would be at Bedloe about half-past three or a little later. Would that be all right?

Rollison assured them that it could not be better and was ushered hospitably into the mess where he was fed on bacon, egg and strong tea, in company with a dozen members of the station personnel, the crews of two bombers who had just returned from a 'flip over the pond.' Their desultory talk about the night's journey intrigued Rollison who saw that their tired eyes were bright enough to reveal the spirit in them and wondered whether Gerald Paterson would be anything like them. He asked whether anyone knew Paterson and the men stared at him, suddenly interested in a man who until then had been a chance guest whom there were too tired to worry about.

'Good Lord, yes,' a tall, dark-haired man said. 'Don't we all? Mad blighter.' There was a general chuckle which Rollison rightly took to be praise and appreciation of Paterson. 'He got back last night with a couple of holes in his belly and only just holding together but he got back. Know him?'

Rollison felt a lump hardening in his throat.

'I was going to see him, but—'

'No need to get worried,' a chunky man

224

assured him with a side grin. 'Pat's all right, no holes in his diaphragm. Belly applies to his kite.' His grin widened at Rollison's obvious relief and he went into some details of the escapades for which Gerry Paterson had made himself famous.

It was when the party had left the mess that a broad-shouldered man with the two thick and one thin stripes of a Squadron Leader approached him somewhat diffidently and asked casually:

'Did I gather that you were going to see Paterson?'

'That's right,' said the Toff.

'H'm. Good fellow. You don't know him well, I suppose?' He eyed the Toff as the latter shook his head and then shrugged. 'Oh well. Look here, I shouldn't say this but he's not in any bother? Odd, I mean, you coming up here to see him.'

'No official bother,' Rollison assured him.

'H'm. No. I'd know about that. Or I should. You'll find him a bit tense. Between ourselves, I've often wondered what's on his mind. Not natural, the way he goes on. You expect it in the Polish or Free French boys, y'know, but Pat's got some bug biting him. Best of fellows, flown with me a lot, but—look here, you don't mind me talking like this?'

'Great Scott, no!' exclaimed Rollison, wondering how best to encourage the man to go on talking. He was eager to learn all he

225

could of June's Gerry and it was not yet half-past two; the car would not be ready until three o'clock.

The other car, with the two men it it, was approaching York and a few miles beyond York was Bedloe aerodrome. Neither of them had spoken for some time but both were thinking of the precise instructions they had been given and pondering the chances of being able to carry them out before morning.

'Paterson always gives me the impression that he'll do a dam' fool thing one day and pay for it,' the Squadron Leader commented next. 'Man with a problem, I'd say. I mean, a few nights back—Monday—he dashed down to London. Didn't stay long but came back looking like death. I'd like to help him. If you do learn anything, give me a tip.' He cleared his throat and went on: 'I dropped in here a bit earlier, spot of bother with the kite. My station's Bedloe and I'd like to help Pat, as I say. All this strictly between ourselves, of course.'

'Of course,' echoed the Toff. 'He came to London on Monday, you say?'

'Yes. Good man, thanks a lot.' The Squadron Leader proffered cigarettes, then glanced at the clock. 'Our car won't be long. I'm coming with you. Er—you are Rollison, aren't you? I mean the fellow who gets about one way and the other. Dubbed the Toff, eh?' A slow, shy smile curved the other's lips and he added: 'I thought so, wouldn't have worried you otherwise. I mean, you coming up to see Paterson like this.' He waved a hand uncertainly and smiled more widely. 'Worst of having a reputation. Of course, mum's the word from me. Let's go out and see about that car, shall we?'

A little tensely the Toff agreed and they sauntered into the night. The Toff was trying to digest the disquieting fact that on Monday, the day of the first murders in Chiswick, Paterson had flown to London and returned 'looking like death.' He remembered, too, that an RAF man had been seen near the shop but hurried away.

Fifteen miles away the two men were huddled together in a kiosk and one was saying to an Adjutant at Bedloe:

'If I can have a word with him, I'd be very glad. It's particularly important . . .Yes, I'll hold on, thanks very much.'

CHAPTER NINETEEN

CALLING FLIGHT-LIEUTENANT PATERSON

After a long wait the telephone crackled in the ear of the man from London. He nudged his companion quickly, waited for a man to say

'Hallo' and spoke in a low-pitched, urgent voice:

'Is that Right-Lieutenant Paterson? My name is Edgley and I—'

'I'm sorry, sir,' said the voice at the other end of the wire. 'Mr Paterson is out and isn't expected back for another twenty minutes.'

'Out!' The voice lost much of its culture. 'At this time of night he can't be. He—oh, I see what you mean.' He broke off as in turn he was nudged sharply. 'You mean he's flying. Oh, er—then I'll ring him later.'

'Can I give him a message, sir? Or ask him to ring you back?'

'I won't give him that trouble,' said the man who called himself Edgley. 'I'll call again in about half an hour.'

He rang off and, into the quiet darkness of the kiosk, swore unrelievedly for thirty seconds, finding neither echo nor reproof in his companion. Both of them left the kiosk and went to the car, parked in a nearby field without lights. They lit cigarettes and settled down to wait while above them the air was filled with the droning of aircraft returning from 'flights over Germany.'

At regular intervals the great bombers came, quivering the air and shaking the ground as they drew near and landed. From time to time flares were shown to lead them in and once there was a crash loud enough to make Edgley jump.

'What's that?' he demanded, and peered through the rear window of the car. 'It must have been—say, look at that!'

'Look at that,' commented the Toff as he settled down in the tonneau of an RAF car and, with a girl driving and the Squadron Leader at his side, he contemplated the light which had suddenly appeared in the eastern sky. It was not the beginning of dawn but a red and yellow flare, a streak of flame growing rapidly larger. In the distance the roar of engines could be heard clearly; the operations from the station they were just leaving had been completed before the Bedloe flights and the air nearby trembled less.

'Eh?' asked the Squadron Leader, who had introduced himself as Conway just before climbing into the car. 'Oh, that. H'm. One of them has had a spot of bother. He'll make it.'

To the Toff the complete detachment of flying men had always been a thing of wonder and it grew no less then as he watched the streak of flame growing nearer. It was an aircraft returning and the familiar radio phrase 'one of its engines caught fire' was vivid in his mind. He had seen the same thing a hundred times in the first battle of Libya and, although at that time he had grown used to it, he had never ceased to marvel at the coolness of the men who handled burning machines with precision and competence which made courage take on a new and deeper meaning.

As they drew nearer to Bedloe, so the returning bomber drew nearer to them. The fire in the sky became a great beacon and they could see the tail-end of the flames and picture the nose of the bomber, made a silhouette by the engine fire. The droning roar of engines grew louder, not drowned by the sound of the car engine. Rollison found himself fascinated by the sight but forced himself to turn and peer at the vague profile of Conway's face: the light from the returning 'plane was good enough to show the man's features and the glow in his eyes.

Rollison saw a chance of learning more about Paterson and said quietly:

'You weren't far out in guessing, Conway. I want to see Paterson because his girlfriend is having a spot of bother but I have wondered if he knows anything about it. I'm briefed for her, in a manner of speaking.' Having delivered that half-truth, he went on quietly: 'Has Paterson given you any indication of what's bothering him?'

'Afraid not,' said Conway. 'Something eating at his vitals, you know what I mean. Not uncommon, of course. Fellows whose people have been bombed out take it hard, sometimes, but I needn't go into that. Paterson hasn't any people except his girl. Haven't seen her but he showed me a photograph. If she'd turned him down or had gone on the loose, I might have put it down to that but she writes regularly. Not much you don't get to know about the other fellow, of course. It's not that and—anyhow, you may find out something. If I can help, say the word.'

'I've been able to get him a few days' compassionate leave,' said Rollison. 'I pulled a few strings. He doesn't know it yet. I'm told he's flying tonight, by the way.'

'Oh, yes, he's out,' said Conway. 'Due back about now, in fact.' As he spoke he turned towards the other window, seeing the great ball of fire which was now so near and low that it seemed as if they could feel the heat from it. That was an illusion for it was six or seven miles away, although few seeing it would have believed that. It flew lower and lower and against it the tall trees of the surrounding countryside, the roofs and chimneys of many cottages, the square outlines of a huge barn, were all shown in vivid relief. About the burning 'plane there was a great radius of light which remained when the fire itself disappeared from sight.

Conway's teeth clamped together and Rollison heard them.

The glow remained enough for him to see the other's profile. Conway's lips were set, his eyes narrowed and he was looking straight ahead of him, rigid and unmoving. For some seconds he did not even draw on his cigarette but, at last, he relaxed and grunted:

'All right, I think. Damn' kites blow up

sometimes.' The red tip of his cigarette glowed as he pulled at it and he added: 'We won't be long, now.'

A few minutes later they passed the open gate of a field where a car was standing but they did not see that, nor the two men from London sitting in it. Then they passed through a tiny village and turned right. Hardly had they left the main road before the car slowed down and figures loomed out of the glow of the headlamps which also glistened on fixed bayonets. A torch was shone on the face of the WAAF driver and then into the tonneau. Rollison already had his special pass out and Conway was recognised. After a brief inspection they passed on.

Half a mile away a dozen or more tiny little black figures were shown against the blazing red of a fire. By it were several small cars and a fire-fighting unit and they could see the men working hard to put out the flames, which were bright enough to show the men's quarters and the other buildings outside which the car stopped. By the door two or three men were standing, all of them in flying kit.

'Who was it'?' asked Conway, as he climbed out.

'Pat,' calmly a voice replied.

'All right?'

'I haven't yet found the ruddy Hun who can really damage me,' said a negligent voice from a doorway. 'You caught a packet, Con, didn't

232

you? I think—what's that?' he added as a voice called: 'Mr Paterson, sir.' 'What's that, telephone at this time of night? All right, I'll come.'

Standing by the car, the Toff caught Conway's arm and spoke *sotto voce*.

'Can you arrange for us to see him without a crowd?'

'Glad to,' said Conway. 'Come on.' He pushed his way through the waiting people with half-jocular comments as he went and passed the open door of the mess-room. From another room Paterson's rather touchy voice was coming as he spoke into the telephone and he said abruptly:

'Where do you say? What time is the train . . . are you sure? All right, thank you, goodbye.'

The *ting!* as he replaced the receiver sounded clear in Rollison's ears. By then Rollison was wondering, as Paterson had done, who had called the man in the early hours of the morning. He had little opportunity for pondering that, however, for Conway pushed open the door of a small room containing two or three tables and writing desks and then called:

'Pat, half a minute.'

'That you, Con?' Paterson came along the passage, his voice tense. 'I say, old boy, I'm in a spot. I simply must get down to London in a hurry. Can't help it and I don't know whether to wake the Old Man for permission or push

233

off. Can you fix it for me if I do?' He completely ignored Rollison, who was taking stock of his man and liking what he saw.

Paterson was tall, spare-boned, good-looking in a rugged and masculine fashion; his photograph did not bring that out properly. His nose was on the short side and rather broad and his eyes were blue, not unlike June's, although a lighter shade. He had fair, crinkly hair and a close-clipped moustache; his mouth was wide and full but well shaped and, Rollison thought, his chin suggested a man who would not sit back while things were happening elsewhere.

'Don't worry about that,' said Conway. 'Your good angel is on the spot, Pat. Colonel Rollison, Flight-Lieutenant Paterson.' Conway's voice grew formal and then he broke again into the jerky sentences which he had used most of the time. 'Here's your man, Rollison. Call me if I can help. Oh, I forgot—there's a 'plane going down south from Batley around five o'clock: you ought to make it if you hurry.'

Rollison had already shown Conway the authority for Paterson's leave and the Squadron Leader nodded and went out, closing the door behind him.

Rollison saw Paterson's eyes widen and then narrow, as if he were recovering from his surprise and beginning to assess his visitor. There was a momentary silence while Rollison judged the best means of approach. Here was a man who had just force-landed after a bombing sortie over Germany, who had flown for miles with one engine burning, landed and got out without turning a hair. To tell him that his fiancée was likely to be put under arrest at any time, and that the police would probably discover the details of a death he himself had caused, was not much to the Toff's liking.

'Well?' asked Paterson, giving the impression that he did not intend to beat about the bush. 'What is this? A man's just 'phoned me to say that a friend of mine is ill—are you on the same errand?' He looked perplexed, clearly unable to understand why two people should take such interest.

'More or less,' said the Toff. 'Paterson, I'm going to give it to you straight, without any frills. I don't know anything about the other call but I suspect that it's an attempt to get you away from here before I see you.' He prevented an interruption and went on quickly: 'No-one is ill, but your fiancée is recovering after an attempt to murder her.'

'June?' said Paterson in a low voice. 'Do you mean June's been attacked?'

'I do. I've just come from her. I persuaded her to tell me all that she could and it included the story of Brett's black case and its contents.'

'You're sure June's all right?'

'She's in no immediate danger.'

'What do you mean by immediate danger?'

235

snapped Paterson.

'I mean that she's being watched by the police and that there aren't likely to be any more attacks,' said Rollison bluntly. He saw the man's lips tighten, his hands bunch together. 'Paterson, June's been trying to get at that box and as a consequence she's implicated in a dangerous business which doesn't exclude her from suspicion of murder. She tried to avoid telling the truth and I've had the devil's own job to make her promise to repeat it to the police. She's told me most of it and made me promise to see you before I pass the whole story on. Trying to keep your name out of it she's gone near to getting herself killed but the case has reached a stage where you can't be kept out. I want you to come down, tell me your story on the way and then come to the police with it. We can arrange details later.'

Paterson eyed him steadily for some seconds and then glanced up at the clock on the wall.

'Come on,' he said. 'We'll only just get that 'plane.'

He led the way out of the room and Rollison caught him up outside, where he was shouting for a car. One was brought immediately and they climbed in as Rollison said:

'Take it easy, Paterson. I want to know something more about that telephone call you

236

had.'

'Oh, that,' said Paterson disparagingly. 'As you say, someone wanted to prevent you and me getting together. Now, when did it start? Just what's happened?'

Rollison said: 'It's too long a story to be told just like that but there are one or two things we can handle right away. But first, I'd like a direct answer. Is it true that Lancelot Brett's case contained the evidence that you killed his secretary?'

'Yes,' said Paterson briefly and, after a pause, went on: 'I suppose I seem to take this damned coolly, Rollison—your name is Rollison?—but I've been worrying about it night after night as I've been out on operations. It's got into me. I'm nervy and irritable, life's just not worth living. I'd pretty well made up my mind to tell the police and get it over. You came just at the crucial moment. Of course there isn't a ghost of a chance of my proving anything against Brett and they'll think it's all a tissue of lies but at least I'll have it off my mind and if I'm hanged—'

'You won't be hanged,' said Rollison with brusque confidence. 'And no man's proof against the law, you know, not even Brett. But I wish I could understand more about the telephone call,' he added slowly. 'I'm not too sure that we'll get by without trouble.'

'Trouble?' asked Paterson.

As he spoke two figures loomed out from the darkness of the side of the road, so close to the car that the WAAF driver pulled up sharply, shooting the occupants forward in their seats. The men who had caused that reached the tonneau doors and wrenched them open while Rollison and Paterson were recovering from the jolt. A torch shone into the tonneau, and one of the men said:

'That's him!'

And he pointed an automatic towards Paterson as the pilot steadied in his seat.

CHAPTER TWENTY

ROUGH TREATMENT

The toff had been half-prepared for trouble and caught a glimpse of the two men before the girl driver. Consequently he flashed his hand to his holster when the car jolted to a standstill. The jolt forced his hand away but he was steadier before the doors were opened and had the revolver ready. He saw the vague shapes of the two men and even caught a glimpse of the gun. His own revolver was pointing towards the other door but he did not let that interfere with his shooting.

He fired twice; the reports were deafening in the confines of the car.

The man outlined against the door gasped as the bullets entered his chest and the second gasp rose to a scream. The shooting and the gasps affected the other man so sharply that his finger stiffened on the trigger.

Paterson, recovering with commendable speed, leaned forward and punched at the pale blur of a face. His man sprawled backwards. The fall made the fellow pull the trigger but the bullet wasted itself in the air and the field beyond.

'Why, you rudd . . .' began Paterson.

It was impossible for Rollison to see what happened, except that there was a flurry of arms and legs. Then he felt the springs of the car relax as Paterson leapt into the road. He had not realised that Paterson could see in the dark much more clearly than he but he heard scuffling and a shout.

Paterson reached the hedge as his assailant bounced against it and gripped the man's wrist. The gun sent another bullet, this time into the road, and then Paterson twisted the wrist so that his victim emitted a single agonised gasp and the gun dropped to the ground.

Then Paterson went for him.

Rollison, climbing out that side for fear the man proved too much for Paterson, was just able to see the movement of the two men, to hear Paterson's grunting and the squelching noises as his punches went home. Gradually, as his eyes grew accustomed to the darkness, Rollison saw that the airman was punching at the other's face with a ruthless energy and precision which soon reduced the man to impotence and gurgling, decapitated appeals for mercy.

A small, scared voice next to Rollison asked: 'Can I help, sir?'

Rollison turned and saw that it was the driver. Her face was lower than his shoulder and he could not see her expression.

'Bless your heart, not yet, but probably later. Just stand by, will you?'

He left her and Paterson, who still wreaked vengeance, and went to the other side of the car. There was no movement from the man he had shot and he bent over him, shining his torch into a pale face. It was also unfamiliar, although he had been prepared to see one of Ibbetson's men. Frowning, he knelt down and explored the man's chest.

The bullets had entered low down on the right-hand side and were not likely to prove fatal, although the man would be in no shape for talking for a long time while, unless he had medical attention quickly, he might die from loss of blood. Rollison made pads of two handkerchiefs to do all he could to stop the bleeding and thought swiftly as Paterson came to join him.

'That swab won't come round for a while,' he growled.

'Mine wants a hospital quickly,' said the Toff and straightened up. 'They must have come by road. I think we'll go on in their car, if we can find it, and send this fellow back to your place with the girl. They can give him the attention he needs there and we needn't miss that 'plane.'

'Good idea,' said Paterson, 'if they've got a car.'

'They have,' said the WAAF in a stronger voice. 'I've just seen it, sir, inside that field.'

'See if you can get it on the road, pointing the way we're going, will you?' asked Rollison. 'Give me a hand, Paterson.'

Between them they lifted the wounded man into the car which they had just left and then the Toff re-fixed the pads to do all he could to make sure that the bleeding was kept to a minimum. As they worked, the engine of the other car hummed noisily and the girl brought it into the road, turning it without difficulty. She came to report and Paterson, who had learned exactly what Rollison proposed, gave her brief instructions. She was to return to Bedloe Station with the wounded man and arrange for him to have prompt medical attention. The police were to be advised and asked to get in touch with Scotland Yard, mentioning the Jameson case.

The girl repeated the instructions promptly and accurately, saluted, turned the big car and started off with her unexpected burden.

'And she didn't turn a hair,' said Paterson. 'You've got to hand it to the girls, these days. I say, what are we going to do with my man? We should have tied him up and sent him back with her.'

'I don't think so,' said Rollison. 'He can travel with us. Do you think there's even a half-chance of getting him on the 'plane and taking him to London?'

'I do not,' said Paterson emphatically.

In fact there was some difficulty in arranging for Rollison and Paterson to travel south on the 'plane, in view of the battered condition of the man they brought with them. The Station Commander considered that, before going to London, they should interview the local police. Rollison contrived to dissuade him, received his assurances that Paterson's man would be taken into custody as soon as the police could be informed and, after asking the SC to give the message about the Jameson case to the local police, Paterson and the Toff entered the machine which took off for the South soon afterwards.

On the journey the Toff told his story.

At times he had to shout because of the noise of the engines but Paterson heard everything and made little comment. When Rollison had finished, the airman inclined his head a little and said, after a long pause:

'June would try it on her own, of course. She's always advised me against it, bless her.

She—' he broke off abruptly. 'You won't want to hear that,' he went on gruffly. 'You know how things are between us. And she's told you the truth, Rollison; there isn't a lot you don't know now, except for the details that make little difference either way.'

'Let's have some about the trouble between you and Brett's secretary,' said the Toff.

'Oh, that.' Paterson drew a deep breath. 'My God, it's been a nightmare! I always suspected Brett of being a pretty nasty customer and then when I met June and learned that he was victimising her and her family pretty badly, I decided to have a shot at finding out more about it. I was working for Lancaster at the time and Lancaster was a business associate of Brett's.'

'Were they good friends?' asked the Toff.

'I don't think there was much love lost between them,' said Paterson. 'They would have cut each other's throats if they'd had the chance but they found it paid better to work together. Actually, Lancaster's all right. He may have put over one or two shady deals but what big business man hasn't? Brett was the rogue. I did a damn fool thing and broke into his office one night. Oh, it's two years ago now. It was fairly easy and I was often there—I managed to nip the key out of the door one day and make an impression. I felt pretty shady, I can tell you!' It was easy to imagine that Paterson was smiling with a touch of bitter

243

ruefulness as he went on:

'Well, I got in. It wasn't Brett's regular office but a place at Chiswick he used for his dirty work. Ryson, Brett's personal secretary, turned up. He was a slimy, soft sort of customer and started bleating about what he would do when the police arrived. I knew damned well that he wasn't going to tell the police but would pass word on to his boss and that between them they would have me pretty well where they wanted me. I knew that Brett and Ryson were blackmailers on a large scale. Following me, Rollison?'

'Clearly,' admitted the Toff. He knew, now, the explanation of the unsolved murder above the furniture shop in Chiswick. The scene of the second crime was not a coincidence.

'Well, he started his beastly hints about this and that and then he said that it would be very useful to know what manner of man I was. He needed a little information which would make June Lancing come to heel. Words to that effect, you know. He had a gun but I don't think it was loaded. He didn't think I'd put up much of a fight, being caught red-handed. Probably I wouldn't have done if June hadn't been dragged into it but I saw red and had a stab at him.'

'Literally a stab?' asked the Toff sharply.

'Good Lord, no! I mean I jumped at him and let him have a right swing. I've done some boxing and I know how to put my weight behind a punch,' said Paterson. 'I wish I could make you see him. He was a thin, scraggy customer with sneering eyes with the lids half-covering them and a long, thin neck with a great Adam's apple which seemed to move up and down in the slime that the fellow mouthed. He was pushing his head forward when I jumped at him and I caught him when his neck was twisted. It was a pretty hefty punch,' added Paterson abruptly. 'You may have read about it. They found him at the office next morning with his neck broken.'

'Phew!' whistled the Toff, involuntarily.

'Well, that's what happened,' said Paterson. 'You can see what kind of a spot I was in, can't you? I'd broken into the place and I knew that if I admitted it and tried to explain what had happened, it wouldn't have convinced a jury of stage-strucks. I mean, look at the case for the prosecution. All my talk of suspecting blackmail and trying to implicate Brett would have looked like so much cheap talk to try to cover myself and there wouldn't have been a recommendation to mercy. Anyhow,' went on Paterson quickly, 'nothing happened—I'd worn gloves, you see, I was pretty careful—and I thought it would die down. Then Brett sent for me. D'you know what that swine told me?'

'Not yet,' said the Toff.

Paterson's voice was thin but it sounded clearly above the noise of the engines.

'There was a recording apparatus at the

245

office and he removed it before the police arrived. So he had a record of all the conversation and could do just what he liked with it. He made me sign a statement which included a *verbatim* account of what had happened and he used threats against June which made me sign it without a squeal. It was then that I told her what had happened.'

'And you've sat on this for two years,' said Rollison.

'What else could I do?' demanded Paterson hotly. 'My case stood or fell by proving that Brett's the swine that he is and I knew I couldn't do it. Then I heard about the black case. June had heard of it—apparently her father and Brett had done "business" together, much the same way that Brett did business with me. The case almost certainly contained my statement. I *did* manage to get into his office one day and destroy the cylinders on which the voices were recorded and I destroyed a lot of others, too,' added Paterson. 'Anyhow, I felt that I was stuck and it got pretty bad. Brett's bled me of close on ten thousand altogether and—oh, well, it had to come out sooner or later. I only wish June had told me what she was going to do. I would have got leave somehow and gone down to help.'

'You've been better out of it so far,' said the Toff with assurance but there was a worrying thought in his mind: Paterson had been to

246

London on the night of the Commando murder. 'Did you interview Brett personally?'

'Oh, yes,' said Paterson. 'No-one else was hiding behind him, if that's what you mean; it was Brett in person. Then he and Lancaster fell out and I fancy Brett had something on Lancaster that made him anxious to get hold of the case. I know there was some trouble, anyhow. As far as I can see, Lancaster has employed Ibbetson and his men to get it. Of course, it doesn't cover Peveril.'

'Did you know Peveril before?'

'Only casually,' said Paterson. 'Not a man I wanted to cultivate. What a solicitor! I wonder who he's working for?'

'Ye-es,' admitted the Toff. 'It's a question that needs answering but I don't think we'll be long before we get the answer. Did you know that Brett left for America on Government business a few days ago?'

'I read something about it in the papers.' said Paterson, 'but it didn't mean much. He'll come back—he always comes back.'

'I'm not so sure that he will, this time,' said the Toff.

Paterson turned his head abruptly. There was little light in the cabin of the 'plane and he could not see Rollison properly; that may have helped to give the edge to his voice.

'What do you mean?'

'I've just remembered a cryptic phrase of Peveril's,' said the Toff. 'It might explain a lot.

247

In fact it might explain everything. And there was something false about Peveril's talk with Ibbetson. It might explain the remark from another angle. The case is working out and I don't think it will be long before we get to the end of it. The one explanation I don't see yet is why on earth Jameson was implicated. And yet—' he paused, and rubbed his chin. 'I suppose it's obvious enough.'

'What the blazes do you mean?' demanded Paterson.

The Toff did not enlarge because he was too busy trying to fit in the odd pieces of the puzzle, pieces which he believed fitted in to make the whole picture. He was still thoughtful and reflective when the 'plane landed at Hendon just after eight o'clock. By then dawn was spreading over the eastern skies and it was possible to see the outskirts of the sprawling mass of London as they lost height. It was also possible to see cars which were drawn up at the aerodrome and, when Rollison and Paterson stepped out, Rollison was not wholly surprised to see Grice and two sergeants standing by the side of one of the cars.

Grice nodded to him. His face looked drawn and his eyes were red-rimmed but tiredness alone did not explain his curtness as he turned to Paterson and said:

'Are you Gerald Charles Paterson?'

'That's right,' said Paterson, stretching

himself after the constriction of the tiny cabin.

'I am a police officer from Scotland Yard,' said Grice, 'and I am charging you with the wilful murder of Mr Lancelot Brett. Anything you say may be used in evidence.' He finished and the plainclothes men ranged themselves on either side of Paterson who stood quite still without speaking, as if stunned. 'Well, Rollison,' Grice went on in the same lifeless voice, 'you've made one of your major mistakes this time.'

'Did you say the murder of Brett?' demanded the Toff.

'Yes,' said Grice, and went on: 'Brett did not leave for America. He was to have done so but was detained and I was not informed. He was killed outside a shop in Green Street, Chiswick, three nights ago, by a man dressed as a Commando sergeant. I needn't tell you much about that but you may not know that two years ago Brett's private secretary was killed on the same premises.' He turned abruptly to Paterson. 'Where did you put the Commando uniform, Paterson?'

CHAPTER TWENTY-ONE

FULL CIRCLE

Paterson made no reply but tightened his lips and then looked at Rollison. Rollison brushed a hand over his forehead then automatically sought for his cigarette-case. He lit a cigarette while Grice's words echoed in his mind; and the first thing that occurred to him was that Paterson had every motive for the murder of Brett and every opportunity also. He resisted a temptation to declare that the charge was nonsensical: that was his reaction to it, in spite of what he knew, but Grice would not make an accusation of murder without good evidence.

Paterson was eyeing him, ignoring the others.

'You're quite right, Paterson,' said the Toff in an easier voice. 'Say nothing, absolutely nothing at all until you've seen a solicitor. I promised June that I'd see her through, with you, and I will.' He smiled a little and flicked the ash from his cigarette. 'I'd feel better about it, Grice, if I'd had a good night's sleep.'

'You weren't alone in missing one,' said Grice abruptly. 'You should have told me where you were going.'

'Oh, no,' said Rollison. 'Then I could only have seen Paterson with the police bias clearly

250

defined; as it was I saw him untrammelled by suspicions.' His smile widened. 'Don't worry too much, Paterson.'

Grice nodded to the plainclothes men and Paterson turned with them and went to the nearest of the three waiting cars. Members of the aerodrome staff were standing nearby, staring at the party. The pilot and crew of the machine which had carried them remained inside the 'plane, staring down at Grice and Rollison and then across at the star pilot of Bedloe Station. It was easy to imagine the news flashing around the aerodromes, astounding those who knew Paterson well.

Rollison looked at Grice.

'Have you a spare seat for me or aren't we on speaking terms?'

'There's room,' said Grice abruptly. 'Come along.'

Rollison waited long enough to offer thanks for the pilot and crew, wished that there was time for some tea or coffee at the mess and then followed the Superintendent to a police car with a sergeant at the wheel. Another police car was just swinging after the first, in which Paterson was being taken away. Rollison joined Grice in the back of the third car, saying as he sank down:

'Why the bodyguard?'

'It might be necessary,' said Grice shortly. 'Paterson is one of many, he's not alone by a long way.'

'Oh,' said the Toff. 'A diffusion of guilt, that's something. Now do you think you could stop regarding me as a leper and tell me what's caused the brainstorm? We've turned the full circle and we're back at the Jameson case but whether you've got the right angle or not is a different matter. I'm going to be surprised if you can prove your case against Paterson but that's by the way.'

'You're going to be surprised,' said Grice acidly. 'This is the first time I've really been angered by you, Rollison. I've known that you've often worked on your own in the past and be damned to the police but I thought you were prepared to work with me. The Lord knows I've given you enough breaks in this case.'

'You've been good,' acknowledged the Toff slowly, 'but you haven't given me many breaks. They haven't been yours to give. I didn't know everything that had happened and I'm sure you didn't but don't run away with the idea that I've been keeping back relevant facts. I haven't. I've worked on some ideas and only once on definite information. That was when I went to see Paterson.'

Grice drew a deep breath, sounding impatient.

'I hope you're not going to insist that the first you knew about the case was in the papers,' he said. 'Peveril's made a full confession.' He uttered that statement sharply and there was a note of accusation in his voice as he turned to look into Rollison's eyes. He saw a blank expression first and then the slow birth of a sardonic humour which riled him; Rollison saw his lips tighten.

'If Peveril has confessed and involved me prior to the newspaper stories of the man amok, he's found you pretty credulous. Are you telling me that you've arrested Paterson on Peveril's verbal evidence?'

'Once Brett was identified and we had the girl's story—I saw her soon after you did—it was easy. Paterson's told her that he killed Brett's secretary, Ryson. His motive for killing Brett is obvious.'

'Not altogether,' said Rollison slowly. Grice frowned, took out his cigarette-case and proffered it; Rollison stubbed out the end of his first cigarette and lit a second. 'So you're going to pretend ignorance, are you?'

'Not ignorance, innocence,' corrected Rollison absently. 'But defending and proving my part isn't going to lead us far, too many urgent matters demand action. Peveril, now— I've formed ideas about Peveril, who has presumably accused me. He was the first man to give me the faintest suspicion that Brett might not be alive. I pretended to Peveril that I knew everything there was to know about the case and made a comment about Brett going overseas. His attitude changed then and when I brooded over it I wondered if he knew better.

Apparently he knew that Brett was dead. Peveril tried several other little deceptions, too,' he added. 'He was quite sure that he had me fooled. He told me that Ibbetson and company were working for Sir Gregory Lancaster, he even talked about that to Ibbetson himself. But he knew that I was listening in; I think that was just to register the fact that there was a man named Lancaster and that he, Peveril, wanted it to be thought that Lancaster was going all out to get the black case.' Rollison paused and then added, apparently apropos of nothing: 'Have you had the analysis of a cigarette which I sent through to you?'

Grice had been about to make a comment on the Toff's musing but changed the topic abruptly.

'Yes, I have.'

'Was it free from drugs?'

'It was not. It contained enough powdered arsenic to have made the smoker ill for a week, if nothing worse. Why?'

'Well, well,' said Rollison gently. 'Peveril was very anxious to get me off the stage, wasn't he? Yes, Peveril tried to give it to me,' he added as Grice exclaimed. 'Was that included in his confession? It wasn't? The man's memory must be really bad! Confound it, he should be fair when he's telling the police everything! What other pretty story has he bamboozled you with?' Again he went on before Grice could interrupt. 'It wouldn't surprise me if he hasn't told you that Paterson and June Lancing were working with Ibbetson for Lancaster. That would sabotage Paterson's story, and the girl's, and put them both in the ranks of the villains. The snag is that when you get Ibbetson he might not confirm Peveril's story. I'd say that there was danger in the offing for Ibbetson and his friends. Of course,' went on the Toff, his voice rising sharply, '*of course*, we're getting places.'

'A complete denial of Peveril's statement won't cut much ice,' said Grice. 'It's too circumstantial.'

'It would be, he's a clever customer. I don't know what Peveril's told you. Remember, I'm working up the story I would present in his position from what little knowledge I have of his attitude in general. I assumed that Ibbetson or one of his men had killed Fred in the bath, to prevent the possibility of a squeal, but it could easily have been one of Peveril's *aides*. It doesn't do to assume that Peveril's the lone agent he makes out to be. Supposing he was working on the lines of pushing all the blame on to Ibbetson? He started doing it with me, most impressively. He'd know that in a showdown the Ibbetson evidence would be too strong for him, so he'd have to get rid of all support of it. Fred goes first, the others will follow when he or his *aides* have a chance. Unless, of course, the police do some arresting

255

first. They're good at arrests.'

'The last defence of a man outwitted is sarcasm,' said Grice coldly. 'We've picked up one of Ibbetson's men, a Charley Day. He doesn't know a lot and he's neither confirmed nor denied Peveril's story or any part of it. He doesn't know for whom Ibbetson is working but Peveril does. Sir Gregory Lancaster,' added Grice slowly, 'is under arrest. He hasn't talked: he's like you, careful enough to send for a solicitor. But the outlines of the case are clear enough, Rollison. Brett and Lancaster were business associates who fell out. Brett kept powerful evidence against Lancaster in the little black case—as well as evidence against Paterson, the girl's father—who was involved years ago in Company frauds—and a lot of other people. Lancaster employed Ibbetson to get that evidence. Ibbetson succeeded but the girl stole the case from him.

'Meanwhile Brett, who was to have gone to America, heard of what was happening and stayed behind. He was, as we've gathered from June Lancing, a blackmailer and swindler on a large scale and he had his unofficial headquarters above a furniture shop in Chiswick. Paterson had an appointment to see him outside the shop at six o'clock in the evening, three days ago. Paterson dressed himself up as a commando in Jameson's clothes—borrowing them because Jameson was playing with the idea of deserting. They were borrowed with the help of the girl, who looks on the Jamesons as old family servants who will do anything for her. She was a party to the attempt to frame young Jameson. She and Paterson between them arranged for the car to be stranded near the canal and the evidence to lead to Jameson. You swallowed that whole,' said Grice, still unbending.

'Hook, line, and sinker,' admitted the Toff. 'Go on, it's quite a story.'

'I'll go on,' said Grice coldly. 'Ibbetson was at hand as an accomplice—you did suggest that. All of them were working for Lancaster. There may or may not be some truth in the fact that both Paterson and June Lancing believed Brett had blackmailed and/or swindled them or their parents. That's probably the motive for them linking up with Lancaster but behind it all is the fact that Lancaster was afraid of the information Brett could lodge against him, and wanted Brett killed—he was one source of the information—and the evidence destroyed. He used Paterson, knowing Paterson's hatred for Brett. We haven't yet found what roguery Lancaster was involved in but we will now that he's under arrest. His offices and flat are being searched.'

Rollison pursed his lips before saying:

'You didn't arrest Lancaster just on Peveril's evidence. I know that for a policeman you're inclined to take chances but you wouldn't take one like that. So far you've grounds for suspicion, nothing more, and you've too many motives.'

'Peveril had letters, signed by Lancaster, addressed to Ibbetson and giving him instructions to get the case from Brett at all costs. Lancaster was confronted with the letters and his reaction was such that a detention on suspicion was justified,' Grice told him shortly. 'I have been in the police force long enough to know what is strong enough evidence for arrest and what isn't.'

'Oh, of course,' said the Toff off-handedly. 'I know you're quite a policeman. Odd, I haven't met either Brett or Lancaster. These things get out of hand when you're dealing in names and not personalities. So that's the best you can do?'

'Can you do better?' demanded Grice tartly?

'No-o,' admitted the Toff. 'Not yet, at all events. But one thing and its corollary stick out a mile, old man.' He was mild-voiced, friendly and earnest. 'What is Peveril's part in this affair? How has he white-washed himself? And the corollary—in order to save himself and those for whom he's working, he must get rid of all witnesses who can break his story. I mean Ibbetson and the others. They're not a nice bunch and I'd gladly see them dead but they're important witnesses.'

'Peveril's story doesn't exclude himself,' said

258

Grice. 'He has mishandled some clients' money—I suppose I needn't remind you that he's a solicitor?—and Brett knew of it. Peveril wanted the case to destroy the evidence against him. His story to you of having an offer of five thousand pounds for it was all my-eye-and-Betty-Martin.'

'I wonder,' said Rollison gently. 'I wonder a lot. By the way, since Paterson and June Lancing were working with Ibbetson,'—he made the words sound sardonic and absurd—'why did Ibbetson dump her into the canal? Or didn't Peveril know about that?'

'She met Ibbetson at the cottage by arrangement, sent the older Jamesons out for the evening and then, I imagine, quarrelled with Ibbetson, who was the only man who knew that Paterson had flown down from his Yorkshire station on the afternoon of the murders and back the same night—using the same means of transport as you. I've checked up with the authorities. Paterson was away that day. Jameson has been released,' added Grice. 'He's going back to his unit at once. You were right about him, anyhow.'

'I see,' said the Toff gently. 'I *see*. You think that Ibbetson and the girl quarrelled, the girl lost her head and started threatening and Ibbetson thought what a good idea it would be to drop her into the cold waters. It's plausible but the operative word you used is "imagine." You shouldn't imagine so much, it's bad for a policeman. Anyhow, as far as you're concerned everything in the garden is lovely?'

'It is,' said Grice; and then sharply: 'There's a lot to be discovered yet but we have all the people who matter, apart from Ibbetson and he'll be picked up soon.'

'I wonder,' said the Toff, as the car slowed down outside Scotland Yard, 'I wonder if I'm just a damned fool or whether the evidence has been neatly planted against Paterson and his girl? I wonder if those two aren't victims of circumstantial and *prima facie* evidence, suffering the tortures of damnation after years of the agony of suspense? I wonder if Peveril isn't going to get away on a negligible charge of embezzling and then come out to enjoy all the proceeds of the job, the real job that's been done? Grice, if you've got a conscience and want it to rest easy in your dotage, be careful now. Spread yourself as you've never done in the past *and pull Ibbetson in before Peveril's other men get him.'*

As he spoke the Toff opened the door of the car, held up by a police van in front of it and almost stationary. He nodded but his expression was bleak enough to startle Grice as he stepped from the car, swayed to regain his balance then turned and walked swiftly towards Parliament Street as the car moved forward.

CHAPTER TWENTY-TWO

FULL TRUTH

Rollison hurried up the stairs to his flat, making little noise and taking his key from his pocket as he went. He did not exclude the possibility of being attacked but as his key turned in the lock he heard Jolly's voice from the reception lounge:

'I won't be a moment, sir.'

Jolly's footsteps followed and thereupon there was the sound of the bolt being drawn. Jolly opened the door and stepped aside for the Toff to enter, closing the door again but this time not bolting it.

'I thought it wise to take every precaution, sir.'

'You're always wise,' said the Toff and meant it. 'In fear of assault, Jolly, or just nerves?'

'The circumstances indicated extreme caution,' replied Jolly. Like the Toff's his eyes were red-rimmed, ample evidence that he had not slept a great deal the previous night. 'I cannot be sure that I was not followed from The Bargee, sir, while the policeman you sent to inquire about me mentioned my name in the saloon and it may have been associated with you. I haven't been back very long,' added

Jolly apologetically, 'but I've just made some tea—would you like a cup?'

'Many cups, yes. I'll be ready in three minutes.'

It was obvious that Jolly had news he considered to be important but Rollison felt in need of a refresher before learning what it was. He went into the bathroom and washed his hands and face in tepid water and, while drying himself, walked into the lounge where Jolly was depositing a tea tray and some cold toast on a small table—not bought from Harridges.

'Good,' said Rollison and took a cup. 'Very good, Jolly. Now don't sit on it any longer. What happened?'

Jolly said slowly:

'I *think* Ibbetson and two of his accomplices are at The Bargee, sir. I waited until a little before closing time and then I—er—I forced entry.' Jolly sipped his tea and went on in a quick, almost excited voice for him. 'It wasn't very difficult and I managed to look in most of the rooms before I was heard. Then I heard someone say "Gibby".'

'Ibbetson's nickname, yes,' said the Toff sharply, his tea momentarily forgotten.

'Then there was an oath and another man— probably Ibbetson, I thought—distinctly said: "That's Peveril, the swine." I did not stay much longer,' admitted Jolly, 'but I was there long enough to understand that they were afraid of

Peveril and at the same time prepared to murder him if the opportunity arose. At all events, sir, I managed to get outside and from a nearby house watched the others looking for me. Five men left the inn—it would be about half-past twelve when that happened—and after about twenty minutes the first returned and the others followed. I can't be sure that they were the same men but I heard "Gibby" mentioned again and presume that Ibbetson was with them.'

'What then?'

'I waited nearby and watched the inn, sir,' said Jolly, 'after telephoning Sammy Diver and asking him if he could send a couple of men to help me. He promised that he would and they arrived soon after four o'clock. I waited a little longer and then returned here in the hope that you would be back. I told the men that they were to telephone here if anyone left The Bargee and that one of them was to follow. I did wonder afterwards whether I would have been wise to ask Diver for more than two men.'

'Two should do,' said the Toff. 'Ibbetson won't leave that hidey-hole unless he's forced out. The trouble is that Peveril's men might find a way of getting in.' He finished his tea and poured out a second cup, crunching a piece of toast as he did so, told Jolly the essentials of his story and added: 'You learned nothing else?'

'Nothing, sir. But a few minutes ago a man telephoned. I liked neither his voice nor his manner but he said that Ibbetson would be leaving The Bargee at ten o'clock this morning!'

'Did he, by Jove,' said the Toff slowly. 'We'll ponder over that. Now you've done better than I hoped,' he said warmly, 'and we should be able to make it. Jolly, we'll see this thing through ourselves; it isn't safe to leave it to others.'

'Meaning the police.' murmured Jolly.

'I'm not in favour with the police just now. Peveril has convinced them that I've been working for Paterson and June for some time. Grice thinks that I've taken a quixotic interest in the couple and that I'm backing their innocence against all reason. Very carefully Peveril has convinced Grice that for once I'm a danger to a successful police action, rather than a help to them achieving it, and Peveril has a considerable degree of low cunning. Why hasn't he been to The Bargee? He certainly knows about it.'

'Did you tell me that he was under arrest, sir?' asked Jolly discreetly.

'There are others working with Peveril, he's not on his own. And what they will want to do is to offer further "proof" that I've been in it all the time and thus strengthen their contention that I've been helping Paterson and June for longer than I've pretended. Also, they will almost certainly prefer me to get into a jam, Jolly. For instance, they will expect me to go to The Bargee, to see Ibbetson. They telephoned a message for me, didn't they? On my arrival they'll break in or follow me in. Violence is likely and, if their plans don't go awry, Ibbetson and the other witnesses will be silenced. And—*and*,' continued the Toff very tensely, 'they will shape the evidence to make it look as if I did the silencing.'

'Are you serious?' ejaculated Jolly.

'Of course I'm serious,' said the Toff sharply. 'From the time that I saw young Jameson I've been the Aunt Sally. All the evidence and most of the actions have been turned against me: the major effort of the other side has been to switch police attention to me. It's been done well. Grice is more than half-convinced. Our question is: who has worked with Peveril and who conceived the idea in the first place?'

'Have you any idea, sir?' asked Jolly faintly.

'A glimmering,' admitted the Toff. 'No more than a glimmering and, if it grows into a bright light, we'll have deserved most of what's happened for being too free with our sympathy. Or I will,' he amended hastily. 'Now, if I'm right—and please God I am!' he exclaimed with unaccustomed fervour '—the flat is being watched. I shall be followed. You'll follow my follower. And I think—'

He paused, then stepped across to the

265

telephone and dialled a number in Aldgate. In a few moments he was talking to a Mr Samuel Diver, who kept a large and prosperous public house near Aldgate High Street and who was indebted to the Toff for several particular favours. Amongst Sammy Diver's various activities there was the running of a gymnasium in the Mile End Road, a chopping-block for ambitious boxers, a rendezvous for the hundreds who had battled in the ring and passed their heyday. The Toff, in peace time, had been a regular patron of the gymnasium and knew most of the members of Sammy's club. Jolly, knowing that, had called upon the man for help and the Toff obviously considered the idea worth imitating, for he asked Sammy for another four or five men who were to go to The Bargee and to wait nearby.

Sammy promised gladly that he would arrange that at once.

The Toff replaced the receiver, lit a cigarette and then nodded slowly. Although he looked as tired as he felt, there was a gleam in his eyes and a sense of satisfaction within him which rendered him oblivious to the chance of being proved wrong. He would have denied emphatically that he was working a hunch: that he had been framed carefully and cleverly from the beginning—his beginning—of the affair was obvious and he considered the last act in the framing a natural consequence of

266

the earlier ones.

'Are you ready to start, sir?' asked Jolly.

'I've had some second thoughts,' the Toff told him. 'You and I will go together. We'll both be followed and our man or men will think that it's working out very nicely. And why shouldn't it?' he added for no reason at all. 'We'll go slowly to The Bargee, getting there after Sammy's reinforcements have arrived. Our follower probably won't think of reinforcements in the form of Sammy's men, he'll be on the lookout for police, not bruisers.' He thrust his hands into his pockets, hesitated and then stepped to the window. He saw nothing to interest him in the Terrace and turned to say quietly: 'If you wanted to murder three or four men, all of whom could provide evidence against you, what would you do? Assuming,' he added, 'that the men were likely to come out of a house or a shop or even a pub together.'

Jolly considered for a while, and then said: 'I don't quite follow you, sir.'

'Don't you?' asked Rollison softly. 'Think again, Jolly. Think back to the newspaper stories we read about the Chiswick murder, and . . . I see you've got it,' he added softly. 'I see you've got it.'

Jolly eyed him for a moment in amazement and then with a dawning apprehension. They were silent for a while, before Jolly said as softly as the Toff:

'You think they'll try the madman-with-a-gun trick again, sir?'

'It certainly wouldn't surprise me,' declared the Toff. 'Come on, let's get over there.'

They left the flat a few minutes afterwards and walked to Piccadilly, going down to the Underground station. As they walked they were careful not to look behind them or to give the slightest impression that they suspected that they were followed; but they were followed by a man in the uniform of a Commando with the three stripes of a sergeant on his sleeves.

*　　　*　　　*

The Toff and Jolly reached The Bargee at five minutes to ten. The public house was on the corner of two narrow roads, a dingy little place with boarded windows and a dilapidated sign hanging outside. A frowsy woman was swilling the pavement outside the pub with dirty water. Rollison and Jolly passed on the other side of the street, walking casually but seeing three of Diver's men within easy distance.

Rollison ignored them, whispering to Jolly:

'Wait here for a moment.'

He went on, turning a corner and seeing a fourth of Sammy's men waiting near it, apparently interested in the window of a confectioner's shop. Rollison spoke before he reached the man, to receive a shake of the head which suggested that nothing of interest had happened. Rollison continued to speak, not raising his voice but uttering the words loudly enough for the other to understand.

'Tell the others to watch for a car, which will probably pull up opposite the pub, and stop anyone who goes towards it.'

'Oke,' came a gruff response.

'Thanks,' said Rollison and then turned and sauntered back, glancing at his watch as he turned the corner and seeing that it was three minutes to ten. The need for keeping away from the front door of The Bargee was obvious but the temptation to go there was strong. He saw Jolly strolling along the road thirty or forty feet away while the minute hand of his watch crept round and he saw that only one minute remained. The possibility that the message had been telephoned to get him there while action was staged elsewhere made him uneasy but then he heard the sound of a car engine approaching from a nearby road and unfastened the flap of his holster, taking a grip on his revolver.

The car turned the corner. It was an open one and he did not recognise the man at the wheel. But he did recognise the man in khaki with a *Commando* tag on his shoulder who suddenly appeared in the porch of a house alongside the hotel.

As the man appeared the hotel doorway opened and a man glanced quickly up and

269

down the street. Rollison, the Commando and Jolly were all hidden from his sight. The man peered at the car, which was driven past at a fair speed, then backed into the pub. A moment later he reappeared with two companions. Despite greasepaint and dirt smeared over the face of one of them, Rollison recognised Ibbetson. He imagined that one of the others was 'Mike.'

Rollison stepped into sight and started to go across the road. The Commando advanced suddenly and in his hands there was a small machine-gun of the type used by the British shock troops. He levelled it as Rollison neared the party coming from the hotel and while Ibbetson, seeing the Toff, turned and began to run.

Quite calmly, Jolly fired his automatic at the Commando.

The single shot from his gun echoed sharp and clear in the crisp morning air. The Commando gasped and half-turned; there was blood on his right hand and the automatic machine-gun drooped towards the ground. He made a quick, desperate effort to regain it but Jolly fired again.

Ibbetson and the others were running full pelt towards the nearest corner. The man at the wheel of the small car was in the middle of turning in the road. He glanced over his shoulder and his expression held horror and dismay. Rollison divined his intention of getting away while the chance remained and fired towards the car; his second bullet punctured a rear tyre which exploded with a loud report. The car slewed across the road then crashed into the kerb and against the brick wall of a small house. As it crashed, Ibbetson and the others reached the corner and then ran into the arms of Sammy's men, taken so much by surprise that they did not even put up a fight. Had they done, two more of Sammy's men, hurrying towards the scene, would have stopped them.

The Toff and Jolly turned towards the wounded Commando, whose gun was on the ground and who was leaning against the wall of the house where he had taken shelter, his face twisted in pain. Everything had happened so swiftly and been carried out with such assurance that Jolly's mild question was an anticlimax.

'Do you know him, sir?'

'Oh, yes,' said the Toff. 'I told you that my sympathies had been working too freely. That's young Jameson but his second attempt wasn't as successful as his first. I think we'd better 'phone Grice now or he'll lose patience.'

CHAPTER TWENTY-THREE

WITHOUT FRILLS

On the way to Scotland Yard, in company with several of Grice's men, were Jameson, Ibbetson, Mike and the landlord of The Bargee whom Jolly knew but who was a stranger to the Toff. With them was the driver of the car which had been intended for Jameson's getaway, on exactly the same arrangement as Ibbetson's car had been used during the attack at Chiswick.

Grice's men were questioning the rest of the staff at The Bargee while the Toff, Grice and Jolly stood together in the small parlour of Canal Cottage. In the kitchen the little woman was weeping piteously and young Jameson's father was trying to comfort her.

Convincing evidence had been found in Jameson's room to prove that he had worked with Peveril and several other men—including the car driver and the couple who had tried to attack Paterson near the Bedloe Station. One of them, young Jameson had admitted, had killed Fred at the Vauxhall Bridge Road apartments.

'And now we have the whole story without frills,' said the Toff quietly. 'The question that worried me most was motive. I could believe in a young couple like Paterson and June Lancing trying to destroy evidence which might send one of them to the gallows but I couldn't believe that several different parties all wanted the case for the same reason. Peveril and Ibbetson were obviously separate organisations, both after the black case. I wanted to know why and made a guess.'

'Go on,' said Grice quietly.

'If the contents of that case were what June Lancing told me, it was worth a fortune to any man unscrupulous enough to use the evidence Brett had gathered as a means of extorting money. That simple motive seemed to me the most likely: Ibbetson and Peveril, both rogues of some cunning, both confident of their ability to work the racket as well as Brett, probably knowing about the case because information against them was inside it, wanted the contents for just that reason. With it they could make money to their heart's content. But of course Brett would object. He did but they knew that he did not leave for America and with Jameson's help they killed him.

'June Lancing had confided in the Jamesons, her old servants, and the parents had no idea of their son's part in it, so they passed the news on. June doubtless told them that Paterson was to meet Brett outside the Chiswick shop—she knew the interview had been arranged, that Brett had sent for Paterson to discuss further payments. The idea

273

of the man running amok seemed a sound one. They used it to good effect but, when it seemed possible that Jameson would become implicated, he worked up a pretty story which, for a time, convinced me. I wasn't sure of Jameson until I saw him this morning but I had been thinking of him for some time. You see, his parents apart, Jameson was the only man who could have spread news both to Peveril and June Lancing that I was working. Ibbetson, of course, learned it from Peveril. Peveril checked it up by forcing June to tell him the whole truth and, as June had sent me the case, he let her go free.'

'I see,' said Grice slowly. 'And Jameson has made a statement?'

'He has and Ibbetson has confirmed a lot of it. Peveril's other man, who was the car driver this morning, admits to having sent two men to kill Paterson last night. Jolly took notes in shorthand,' added the Toff, 'but I don't think you need worry, you've got everything now. The simple motive,' he added slowly. 'The value of the black case was the information in it; they wanted the information, not to save themselves but to use it as Brett had done. Peveril tried to hoodwink me by talking of getting five thousand pounds for it and by trying to persuade me that Ibbetson was working for Lancaster. I doubt whether Lancaster knows anything about it; those letters were probably forgeries.'

'Ye-es,' said Grice and pushed a hand through his hair. That's his contention anyhow. He is nervous in case I press the charge too far. I think he has plenty to hide.'

'I doubt whether you'll get anything against him but that's up to you,' said the Toff. 'Brett had plenty, in the case, but we know what happened to that. It's odd,' he added thoughtfully. 'Brett died before I heard of him and I haven't met Lancaster. The hierarchy of big business evaded me. I would have liked a cut at them. However, it didn't work out that way,' he added with a crooked smile. 'Will you look after everything and let Paterson and June know what's what as soon as you can? You'll want to verify everything before you release them, of course, but ask them to go to my flat when you've finished.'

'I will,' promised Grice and then added with some embarrassment: 'Rolly, I feel badly about this. I should have known better than—'

'Hush!' exclaimed the Toff. 'A policeman never apologises!' He rested a hand on Grice's shoulder and added: 'I'm glad it worked the way it did. The first real glimmering came when I saw a possible source of the rumour that I was deeply involved in the affair. And when I remembered that June Lancing had learned it from the Jamesons, because of my visit—'

He shrugged while the crying woman in the next room grew quieter and her husband's

275

tones grew softer and still more soothing. Rollison did not like what had happened to them and yet there was nothing he could do to offer comfort. But he told them to call on him for anything they needed and then went to the nearby houses and redeemed his promise of ample compensation to Mrs Mee and even more generously rewarded the less avaricious Good Samaritan next door.

Jolly went ahead of him to the flat and Sammy Diver's men, satisfied with their brief appearance, were on the way to Aldgate.

Rollison strolled along the canal thoughtfully, thinking of the desperate lies June had first told him, of her story of being an alien related so plausibly and, like that of Jameson, once deceiving him. His chief anxiety was that Gerry Paterson might face a charge of the murder of Brett's secretary and, before he returned to Gresham Terrace, he interviewed a rotund little man in the Public Prosecutor's office, who shook his head sorrowfully after he had heard the story of Paterson's confession—without learning names—and said:

'Rollison, my boy, you're not yourself. *If* all the evidence is hearsay, *if* there is none stronger than that, if everything that we could use in court was destroyed in that black box and when Brett died—why, there isn't a case. The youngster's made a confession, you say?'

'To me, not the police.'

'Then tell him to keep quiet. Tell Grice

276

yourself and let Grice work it out. I don't think he'll want to prefer a charge. I'm quite sure any barrister could get a "not guilty" verdict even if he sent it to court. Your young friend hasn't much to worry about.'

In a much more cheerful frame of mind, the Toff returned to Gresham Terrace. Outside the flat a plainclothes man was waiting; inside were June and Paterson. He assured himself quickly that June had told the police everything except Gerry's encounter at Brett's office.

'Of course I didn't tell them that!' exclaimed June. 'I'm not quite mad. And in any case it wasn't deliberate, it was accidental. You yourself said it would be reduced to a manslaughter charge!'

'So I did,' smiled the Toff, 'but it needn't go as far as that, if you watch your step. Grice has put a man to watch you but he has to do that until everything is over.' He glanced at his watch and his eyes widened. 'We've just time for some lunch and then I must get to the office. We'll go out for it. Jolly, will you have a holiday and come with us?'

'I think I would prefer to stay here, sir, thank you,' said Jolly and later watched from the window as they walked along the Terrace.

We hope you have enjoyed this Large Print book. Other Chivers Press or Thorndike Press Large Print books are available at your library or directly from the publishers.

For more information about current and forthcoming titles, please call or write, without obligation, to:

Chivers Large Print
published by BBC Audiobooks Ltd
St James House, The Square
Lower Bristol Road
Bath BA2 3BH
UK
email: bbcaudiobooks@bbc.co.uk
www.bbcaudiobooks.co.uk

OR

Thorndike Press
295 Kennedy Memorial Drive
Waterville
Maine 04901
USA
www.gale.com/thorndike
www.gale.com/wheeler

All our Large Print titles are designed for easy reading, and all our books are made to last.